TO LOVE A BEAST

ONCE UPON A TIME IN TEXAS
BOOK ONE

KAREN WITEMEYER

HOPE & LIGHT
PUBLISHING

Books by Karen Witemeyer

<u>Novels</u>

A Tailor-Made Bride
Head in the Clouds
To Win Her Heart
Short-Straw Bride
Stealing the Preacher
Full Steam Ahead
A Worthy Pursuit
No Other Will Do
Heart on the Line
More Than Meets the Eye
More Than Words Can Say
At Love's Command
The Heart's Charge
In Honor's Defense
Fairest of Heart
If the Boot Fits
Cloaked in Beauty
To Love a Beast

<u>Novellas</u>

A Cowboy Unmatched
Love on the Mend
The Husband Maneuver
Worth the Wait
The Love Knot
More Than a Pretty Face
An Old-Fashioned Texas Christmas
Inn for a Surprise
A Texas Christmas Carol
In Her Sights

To all book-loving heroines in the real world.

May your hunger for knowledge feed your intellect,
and may your thirst for story stir your empathy for
others even as it fills your heart with joy.

A new heart also will I give you, and a new spirit will I put within you: and I will take away the stony heart out of your flesh, and I will give you an heart of flesh.
Ezekiel 36:26

Prologue

New York City, 1886

Everett Griffin strutted through the halls of the Union Club like a thoroughbred stallion on the auction block—for that's what he was. New York's Golden Boy. The American Adonis. The bachelor who would barter his handsome face along with his freedom for the right price. A very *high* price.

Everett's mother had made no secret of her desire for the Griffins to take their place in the vaulted Four Hundred alongside the Astors and Vanderbilts. However, wealth alone wouldn't open that door. One needed connections and acceptance. Hence the strutting and ingratiation Everett engaged in on a regular basis. Mother insisted that if God had made Esther beautiful so she could become a queen and protect her people, then the Lord must have similar plans for Everett, for no man had been blessed with a finer countenance. It was his duty to use his God-given beauty to marry royalty just as Esther had done. And the Four Hundred were New York royalty.

Everett had yet to deduce what dire fate he was supposed to be saving his family from. He doubted genocide was on the table as it had been for the Jews of Esther's time. Although, the way Mother carried on, he wouldn't be surprised if she equated ostracism from the top tier of society to death in some way. Death of a dream, he supposed.

Not that he resented being thrust into the role of family savior. He rather liked the idea of playing hero. And what hotblooded male didn't enjoy having young, beautiful women constantly seeking his attention? Not to mention the fact that placing himself on the marriage mart allowed him to delay taking up the expected mantle of working in his father's investment firm.

He'd not inherited his father's love of ledgers. That privilege belonged to his older brother, Alex. Stuffy offices filled with stock reports, business journals, and other people's accounting information held no appeal for Everett. He'd rather pour his energy into art, music, and literature. Creation stirred his passion. Beauty tugged at his soul. It was probably why he was so much closer to his mother than his father.

Bradley Griffin considered the arts nothing more than a hobby and constantly urged Everett to set aside his toys and do a real man's work. Mother, on the other hand, had nurtured his talent since she'd first seen him sketch a lopsided bowl of fruit at the age of six. A rather accomplished watercolorist herself, she'd trained him in the arts of perspective and proportion, texture and movement, color and form. When he decided he preferred the more robust layering and depth available in oils, she hired an instructor to educate him in that medium as well. Then, last year, when she deemed him ready, she arranged for a local gallery to display and sell a few of his pieces. He might not possess an aptitude for banking, but he was not without his talents.

As Everett strolled through the Union Club's reading room, making small talk with various acquaintances, older gentlemen with cigars and cognac stole glances at him. Some scowled their disapproval at his inclusion in their sanctum, his family's money too new and his ties to European aristocracy too weak to associate with their exalted bloodlines. Yet the wealth his father had amassed working with J. P. Morgan, plus Morgan's personal recommendation, had opened doors and presented possibilities. Those who *weren't* looking at him in disdain, eyed him with either envy or calculation. It was the calculation that brought Everett to the club three days a week. He wooed society's daughters at various balls and dinner parties, but he wooed their fathers at the club.

"There he is. The Face that Launched a Thousand Skirts." George Childers chuckled as he clapped Everett on the back and steered him toward the billiard room where a handful of young men had gathered to watch a game currently underway. "Hey, fellas. Look who grew tired of being besieged by young ladies and decided to take refuge in a more masculine domain."

A chorus of moans sang through the room, accompanied by theatrical eye rolls and a rather menacing glare from a gentleman in the corner who'd taken umbrage with Everett's usurping his waltz with a certain debutante last night.

"Ah, don't let them bother you." George winked as he moved closer to the pool table to get a better view of the game. "Every guy here'd love to be you, Griff. Well, except for me. I aim to hold on to my bachelor status for at least another two years. Your distraction of the female population works decidedly in my favor." George leaned close and elbowed Everett in the ribs. "Don't guess you'd care to give a fella a tip on which female might have caught your eye? Quite a few wagers are making their way around the club regarding which lass will land you. Wouldn't mind profiting from your success."

Walter Donaldson looked up from his cue stick to scowl at them. "Shut up, Childers. I'm trying to concentrate."

Eyes dancing, George held his palms up in mock surrender and backed away from the table.

"I take it he's losing?" Everett made a point to keep his voice low, not wanting to aggravate the situation.

The Donaldsons were clients of his father's firm, and while Everett might not enjoy the management side of the business, he understood the importance of catering to the egos of influential families. If boats rocked, he and his father were the ones in danger of being tossed overboard.

"Already down one game," George confirmed. "Challenged Palmer to a rematch, but it doesn't seem to be going any better than the first." George thumped Everett on the back. "You should stick around. Once Walt clears out, you can give Palmer a run for his money. You're probably the only one in the room who can best him."

"Perhaps another time," Everett said. "I have an appointment to keep."

"Ho! I know that smile." George leaned close. "What's her name?"

Behind all the lighthearted, ridiculous antics, George Childers was a rather insightful individual. It was probably why he and Everett got along so well. They'd both mastered the art of putting up fronts to disguise the deeper machinations going on beneath the surface.

"Lillian March. Her mother has invited me to tea."

"The Enchantress?" George let out a low whistle. "You're going to be the envy of every unmarried man in this club when word gets out. How'd you wrangle a private invitation? From what I hear, she's never at home to gentlemen callers and is rarely seen about town unless in the company of either her father or brother. A rather brilliant ploy—creating an aura of mystery around her to entice the most sought-after bachelors of the season." George lowered his voice and leaned close. "Although . . . I've heard whispers that something is a bit . . . off . . . with the fair Lillian. It seems there's a great-aunt or grandmother or someone who spent time in an asylum back in England." He summoned a soft, airy whistle that floated between them like a specter as he shot Everett a warning glance. Then his affable grin returned to erase the chill from Everett's nape. "I wouldn't worry, though. The story was probably put about by some jealous debutante who didn't wish to share the spotlight with a young lady of such ethereal beauty."

Ethereal was right. Lillian March's silvery blonde hair, fair complexion, and bright blue eyes made a man think of fairies and magical realms. At least that's what came to Everett's mind the first time he'd seen her at a ball over a month ago. But it was when he'd first heard her sing at a dinner party a couple weeks ago that he'd understood why the papers had dubbed her *The Enchantress*. The woman's voice captivated all who listened. She didn't perform with the melodramatic passion of an opera singer, nor did she belt out notes with the confidence of one secure in her own talent. Instead, she sang as if she were the only one in the room, making music solely for her own delight. Sweet, pure tones, almost childlike in their simplicity, had woven through the drawing room on gossamer threads, soft enough that one had to concentrate to hear them. The entire assembly had fallen silent that evening as she cast her spell over the audience.

"My mother arranged the meeting." She'd noted Everett's interest at the musicale and had made it her mission over the last few weeks to worm her way into Mrs. March's good graces. Anthony and Paulette March might be a tad reclusive, but as members of the Four Hundred, they possessed the one qualification Mother prized most of all, social standing. "When Mrs. March learned that I often sketch likenesses at parties, she expressed an interest in having me sketch her daughter. It seems Miss March doesn't care to sit for portraits. If my rendering does the fair Lillian justice, her mother plans to use it as the foundation for a professional portrait."

"Clever." George nudged an elbow into Everett's ribs. "You *will* tell me everything about the lady after your encounter, won't you? I can't think of any one of my acquaintances who has spent more than the length of a single dance in her company. She's a mystery that needs solving."

"Now, Georgie. You can't praise my cleverness then turn around and expect me to do something so foolish as to surrender my advantage to the rest of the field."

George raised a brow. "I was praising your mother's cleverness, not yours."

Everett laughed. "Ouch."

His friend grinned good naturedly and gave Everett a small push toward the door. "Go on. Take that handsome mug of yours and go woo the most interesting debutante of the season. I'll find a way to pull all the details out of you later."

"You're welcome to try." Everett saluted his friend and strolled out of the billiard room.

An hour later, he sat in the March family parlor sipping tea, nibbling cakes, and wondering what in the world he'd gotten himself into. Lillian March kept shooting him glances he couldn't interpret, and every time she opened her mouth, her mother jumped in to steer the conversation. He felt a little sorry for the younger lady. He knew a bit of what it was like to have a parent intent on directing her child's life the way *she* thought it should go. Usually a charismatic smile, a little flattery, and a solicitous comment or two allowed him to win his way into a mother's good graces, but Paulette March remained unmoved by his charm. She had an agenda, of that he had no doubt, but she hid it well.

As lovely as *The Enchantress* was, Everett wasn't sure he could stomach having a mother-in-law as controlling as his own mama. One overbearing woman in his life was quite enough. The few times he'd encountered Lillian March, she'd seemed like a sweet-natured, quiet young lady, if a bit vapid. Her lovely voice made up for her lack of intelligence and spirit, and, if he were honest, he rather liked the idea of having a woman he could easily mold to his will. Her mother was a far different story. There'd be no bending that woman to any man's will. Were he to marry Lillian and a time arose when she had to choose between following her husband's wishes or her mother's, Everett would lay odds on Mrs. March winning that contest every time. A dismal prospect. Best he scratch Miss Lillian's name off his list of bridal candidates.

"Can I pour you another cup of tea, Mr. Griffin?" Mrs. March reached for the white ceramic pot on the tea cart the butler had wheeled in twenty minutes earlier.

Everett leaned away from her, placing a poetic hand upon his chest. "What sustenance need I when surrounded by such beauty?"

He smiled first at Mrs. March, then pivoted to include Lillian. The young woman's eyes glowed with strange light, almost as if they tried to speak on her behalf, though he had no idea what they might be saying. Experience had trained him to distinguish flirtatious glances from shy delight, peevishness from teasing indignation, and wanton invitation from a more innocent interest. The gleam in Miss Lillian's eyes checked none of those boxes, yet it definitely felt impassioned. Almost . . . zealous. An uneasy feeling snaked up the back of his neck, but then the lady blinked and her gaze returned to its rather vacant norm.

Telling himself he'd imagined the odd look, Everett turned back to his hostess. "My mother mentioned that you would enjoy having a sketch done of your lovely daughter. I admit that my fingers itch with the need to set aside this cup and pick up my graphite pencils."

Mrs. March tittered softly, his charm finally finding its way through her armor. "Such a gallant young man." She leaned back from the tea cart and gestured to the art case he'd brought with him. "By all means. Please begin."

Everett set his napkin aside and claimed his oversized sketchbook along with his favorite pencil from the case. He'd considered using charcoal or black chalk, being fond of the deep shading he could achieve with those mediums, but graphite provided the best opportunity for finer detailing and kept one's hands from being covered in black smudges. A decided advantage when surrounded by women and furnishings adorned in fine fabrics.

Mrs. March collected a silver-backed hand mirror from the end table and handed it to her daughter so Lillian could check her hair. Next, Mrs. March turned her attention to ensuring her daughter's dress draped just so. Lillian seemed rather enamored of her reflection, peering into the glass for several moments before her mother snatched the mirror from her hands and returned it to the table. A spark of rebellion flared in Lillian's eyes, but she made no verbal objection. Hoping to clear some of the tension from the air, Everett clapped his hands and smiled when the two ladies glanced his way.

"Never have I had a more beautiful model." One could always count on flattery to unruffle a woman's feathers. It didn't let him down, for both women preened at his praise.

Finally, pencil met paper and personal agendas, manipulative mamas, and concerns about mysterious glances drifted from Everett's mind. His focus sharpened as he concentrated on curves and angles, light and dark, movement and flow. The scratch of pencil on paper filled the quiet room, drawing him deeper into his art. His hand moved over the page in long sweeps followed by shorter, more refined strokes.

Lillian March's face came to life on the paper, the curls of her hair framing her brow while the slope of her shoulders and lines of her bodice grounded the vision like a vase supporting a bouquet. He added some shading to highlight the gentle rounding of her jaw then turned the pencil to its point to shape a delicate nose. Next came the mouth, her lips narrow but well formed, softened in a slight pout he strove to capture. Absorbed in his work, he nearly jumped when Mrs. March broke the silence.

"Lillian, dear. Stop fidgeting with your hands."

The lips he'd been studying so intently pursed in an unattractive scrunch. Lines formed across her brow as well. This would never do.

Glancing around for inspiration, Everett spotted a single rose in a slender vase on the tea cart. He set aside his pencil and sketchbook, stood, and plucked the flower from the vase. After dabbing the stem with a napkin to remove any excess water that might drip upon her dress, he pivoted toward his model and bent in a chivalrous bow.

"May I offer you this rose, my lady?"

Miss March blinked up at him, the lines of frustration erasing from her face. "A rose?"

"A fair flower for a fair beauty." And holding it would give her something to do with her hands while he finished his sketch.

That unsettling look returned to her eyes, making Everett's nape itch, but she reached out and took the stem from him.

"Thank you," she said. "I accept."

He nodded to her then returned to his seat, eager to finish the sketch and take his leave. Concerned more for speed than perfection now, Everett hurried through the last details of her face, leaving her disturbing eyes for last. When he could avoid them no longer, he focused on shape and position, doing his best to ignore the orbs glittering in a way that had him recollecting the rumors of her ancestor's madness.

Movement at the edge of his vision drew Everett's gaze from his sketch. A maid entered the parlor and bobbed a quick curtsy.

"Sorry to disturb, ma'am, but a squirrel got into the kitchen and is running amok. Cook is screeching and threatening to quit. I've never seen her so upset, ma'am. I fear she might suffer an apoplexy."

"Good heavens." Mrs. March scurried toward the door, then stopped and glanced back at her daughter. "I can't leave . . . I . . ."

"I'll stay with Miss Lillian, ma'am." The young maid hurried forward. "Cook needs you."

Mrs. March frowned but eventually nodded. "Do not leave her side, Elsie."

"Yes, ma'am."

Having claimed the maid's promise, Mrs. March turned and fled the room.

Everett lowered his sketchbook. "Perhaps I should take my leave as well. It seems a crisis is afoot."

"Absolutely not." As if her mother's departure had loosed the chains that had heretofore confined her will, Lillian shifted on the sofa cushion, her body vibrating with palpable energy. "Mama has things well in hand. I insist you finish my portrait."

"As you wish." Everett offered a tight smile, wishing it wasn't his duty as a gentleman to see to the lady's needs ahead of his own. "I'm nearly finished, anyway." And was determined to complete the image in record time.

Resuming his work, he turned back to the eyes. He'd just add a few lashes and . . .

"Elsie? I'm growing chilled. Fetch my shawl, please."

Everett's head shot up. No, no, no. He couldn't be left alone with this woman. If someone found them together, he would be expected to offer for her. When he didn't—for nothing could convince him to tie his life to a woman whose sanity seemed questionable and whose mother insisted on controlling every aspect of her life—his chances of marrying into the Four Hundred would disintegrate, and *his* mother would never forgive him.

Before he could offer a word of protest, however, Elsie scurried from the room as if her promise to Mrs. March meant nothing. As if this had been the plan all along. Squirrel in the kitchen. Ha! The girl had probably turned the rodent loose in there herself. Well, Everett wouldn't be playing by their rules. Not anymore.

He closed his sketchbook. "I'm sorry, Miss March, but I must insist I take my leave. You might not be aware, but it is improper for the two of us to be without a chaperone. I will not risk sullying your reputation by staying."

"Wait, please." She leaned across the space between them and clasped his hand, her grip surprisingly strong. "I had to see you alone. Just for a moment." She cast a quick glance toward the door the maid had inconveniently shut then focused again on his face. "I received your message."

Message?

"I think you must be mistaken. I never sent you a message, Miss March."

"You did! At the musicale. Our eyes met as I sang. I saw the music seep into your soul, and I knew at that moment that we were destined to be together."

Everett tugged his hand from hers and gained his feet. "I have a heart for music, and I admit that I enjoyed your song very much, but that is all it was to me—a song."

"Liar!" Lillian lurched to her feet, her eyes blazing. "You told me you loved me. That you would move heaven and earth to be with me."

She *was* mad. "I said no such thing." He retrieved his case. He needed to get out of here. Now.

"Not with your voice," she said. "With your heart. I heard it. In my mind. Just like Jane Eyre heard her beloved Edward call to her heart from miles away."

"*Jane Eyre* is a work of fiction." He fumbled with the strap on his case, his fingers shaking as he tried to get it open.

"It was real. I heard you. And then today, when you offered me this rose, I heard you again." She waved the flower in his face as if it were a magic wand that would make her delusions true. "You proposed marriage—secretly—so Mama wouldn't hear. And I accepted. We are destined to be together, Everett. Forever."

"You misunderstood." The strap finally unfastened. "I did not propose. I'll never propose." Turning his back on her, he flung his case onto the seat of his chair and flipped open the lid. "You are a delightful lady," he said in an effort to appease her wounded pride, "but I'm afraid we do not suit." He tossed his pencil inside, not taking the time to slide it into its protective slot, and shoved the sketchbook in after it.

"Who is she?" Lillian seethed behind him. "Who stole your heart from me? Was it Mary Featherington? I saw you dance with her at the Vanderbilt ball. Or Constance Applewhite?"

"No woman owns my heart," he insisted as he slammed the lid shut.

"You're a disgrace! Toying with women's affections."

Deciding to forgo the strap, Everett tucked the case under his arm and turned to flee. The glint of light on polished silver flashed a second before a heavy object smashed into the right side of his face.

Pain exploded as something cracked beneath his eye. Bone. The art case slid from his grasp. Everett stumbled backward. Tripped over the chair. Blood ran into his eye as he fell, blinding him.

"You beast!"

Another blow, this one slashing like broken glass across his face. He howled as his skin ripped. He turned from the pain, raised an arm to shield himself. But her claws found him, digging into his face like those of a wild animal.

She's going to kill me.

With a wounded roar, Everett raised up and shoved Lillian away from him. He scrambled to his feet, his vision blurred and his balance impaired as he staggered for the exit. Before he could reach the door, however, it flung inward. Mrs. March stood before him, eyes widening in horror.

"Lillian! Stop!"

Something crashed into his skull from behind. The smell of tea engulfed him as he crumpled to the carpet. Hot liquid scalded his face and neck, but the pain lasted only an instant before darkness claimed him.

Chapter 1

Denton, Texas, 1891

"I'm afraid it's broken."

The doctor's pronouncement settled in Callista Rosenfeld's heart like a boulder determined to squash all hope out of her. But instead of sagging at the news, she lifted her chin and straightened her spine.

Touching her father's slumped shoulder, she met the doctor's sympathetic gaze. "How long will his hand take to heal?"

"At least four to six weeks for the bones to mend. Maybe longer due to his advanced age."

Her father's head snapped up. "Advanced age? Bah! I'm not even sixty."

But he would be next spring.

"You're young at heart, Papa. That's what matters most." Callista leaned down and placed a kiss on his bald head. A ring of white hair circled the equator of his skull, fluffing out around his ears in a haphazard manner, as free-spirited as the man himself.

Perhaps a little *too* free-spirited. If he hadn't been tinkering with that hanging pot rack he'd pieced together from scraps of iron the blacksmith had given him, her cast iron skillet never would have snapped the rod and plummeted to crush Papa's hand against the table. She'd told him time and again that she didn't need a fancy rack in her kitchen, that their small cupboard worked just fine. Yet ever since he'd overheard her admiring the rack on display in the hardware store, he'd been determined to build her one. He meant well. He *always* meant well, but he was a bit of a disaster when it came to mechanical operations.

Dr. Haverty met Callista's gaze over Papa's head. "I'll set the bones and apply a plaster of Paris bandage. He's not to use the hand at all, miss. And after the cast is removed, there will likely be some atrophy of the muscles that will require exercises for regaining strength and dexterity."

"I understand."

Papa would not be able to work for several weeks. Perhaps months. Under normal circumstances, such a problem would be a minor hiccup, nothing more. Callista had been taking care of most of the book binding contracts for the last three years anyway. Papa's arthritis made the sewing and detail work difficult for him to manage, though he had a knack for stamp design that Callista would never match. Her father was the artist. She was simply the one who implemented his designs.

If all that was at stake was running their small shop, she'd not be concerned. But far more hung in the balance than repairing textbooks for the North Texas Normal College or handling the occasional request for a decorative rebinding from their wealthier Dallas clientele. They'd been preparing for months to take on the largest commission the shop had ever attempted, using what little savings they possessed to purchase materials and portable equipment for a private library project in a client's home. A client who would not hesitate to seek another artisan book binder if Papa failed to meet his precise expectations.

They'd wagered their entire future on this contract. If they failed to fulfill it, they'd be ruined.

Craving a moment alone to collect her thoughts, Callista left the doctor to his work and stepped into the small room that served as her bedroom. The brave face she'd donned for her father's sake fell away the moment she crossed the threshold of her room. Her hands trembled, and a mist of tears fogged her eyes as she sat on the edge of the bed.

Papa had the smooth tongue to draw in new customers and the artistic eye to create unique designs, but he relied on her to run the logistics of the business. She was the one who ordered supplies, organized their client files, and managed the company finances. Finding a way to salvage this situation would rest on her shoulders.

What were they going to do?

When Papa first received the letter from Mr. Lightfoot, he'd brimmed with excitement. They'd closed the shop early and dined at the café, a luxury they never indulged in since money was always tight. He'd proclaimed the job a gift from God. How else could one explain the arrival of so large a contract from a man they'd never met? A man who could have easily commissioned a more established book binder from Houston or San Antonio for his project. Yet he'd chosen Rosenfeld's Bindery instead. The Lord *must* have seen their poverty and directed his business to their small shop as an answer to prayer.

Only now, in a blink of an eye—or in this case, a smash of a hand—that amazing blessing had transformed into a curse. One that would destroy Rosenfeld's and break Papa's heart.

Hopelessness filled the room like a rushing tide flooding a small cavern. Callista managed to climb out of it when it first wet her feet, but it kept pouring in, now too deep to avoid. The already small room seemed to shrink. Cold seeped into her limbs. Her breathing grew shallow as pressure filled her chest, threatening to drag her into the depths of despair.

Squeezing her eyes closed, she did what she'd trained herself to do as a young girl when she felt overwhelmed. She pictured her mother. Surrounded by wildflowers. The river glimmering behind her. Birds singing. Papa laughing. Mama's hand holding hers.

Callista's breathing slowed. The spinning chaos of her mind slid into the background as she focused on the memory. Her place of peace.

A spring breeze toyed with her hair. Sunlight warmed her face. Waving prairie grass tickled her legs. Happiness danced in her heart. All was well.

All is well here, too.

Callista repeated the admonition in her mind, willing herself to believe it. Just as she had twelve years ago when, at the age of fourteen, she'd sat at her mother's bedside clasping her hand for the last time.

"Hold tight to hope, Callie," Mama had said, squeezing her fingers with what little strength the consumption hadn't drained from her. "The world might seem dark and frightful, but as long as you have hope, you have power. Power to persevere." A cough interrupted, but Mama would not be deterred. She fought through the attack then captured Callista's gaze with an intensity impossible to forget. "Hope sees possibilities where fear sees only barriers. Hope trusts that God will rescue and restore, and it enables us to endure the interim. Despite what people say, hope cannot be stolen or destroyed. It will only be lost if you surrender it of your own free will. So hold tight, Callie. Never let it go."

Callista's hands balled into fists as her eyes slowly opened. "I won't, Mama," she whispered to the empty room, the vow crystalizing in her heart.

If she and Papa could endure losing Mama, they could endure whatever hardship knocked on their door today.

After the doctor left, Callista brewed a pot of tea to share with her father and added a bit of laudanum and honey to his cup to soothe his pain. She drank hers without any sweetening, since the doctor's fee had taken the last of the discretionary funds she kept tucked away in a hollowed-out book in her room. Luxuries like sugar, honey, and jam would not have a place on her shopping list until those funds could be replaced. And with her papa's injury, the replacement of those funds would likely take months instead of weeks. Of course, if they lost the private library contract, affording luxuries would be the least of their worries.

Papa took a sip of his tea, holding the cup somewhat awkwardly with his left hand. He grimaced at the bitterness of the laudanum. Apparently, she'd not stirred in enough honey to mask the taste.

His shoulders hunched as he set down the cup and let out a sigh. "I've failed you, Callie."

"You've done no such thing." She scooted her chair around the corner of the small table to be near him, then laid her head on his good shoulder as her fingers circled his arm. "This is just a minor setback. God will see us through."

"God doesn't suffer fools, and that's exactly what I've been. Thinking we could make a go of a business reliant on a wealthy clientele when we live on the edge of the frontier."

"Denton is hardly the frontier, Papa." Callista smiled and squeezed his arm. "We have the railroad, several hotels, schools, and churches. This area is growing, and you had the foresight to recognize that. Besides, you didn't bring us out here on a whim. You did it for Mama, to get her out of the smoky air of the cities so her lungs could heal. We had time with her we might not have had otherwise, and I'll never regret that. Neither should you."

"Your sweet mama. What would she say about this mess?" He wagged his head, a small nostalgic smile bringing a touch of light back to his face. "Me breaking my hand on the eve of the biggest job of my career?"

"She would have reminded you that God has everything under control."

He chuckled softly. "You sound just like her."

Callista's heart warmed. She could receive no finer compliment.

Papa fiddled with his teacup, his face growing serious again. Deep lines cut into his brow. "I'll have to write to Mr. Lightfoot." He paused, glanced at the plaster bandages encasing his right hand, and grimaced. "I guess *you'll* have to write to Mr. Lightfoot. Explain the situation. See if his employer would be willing to delay the project for a few weeks. It's a long shot, but perhaps the Lord will soften his heart."

Callista straightened away from her father, her heart rate accelerating. Papa couldn't write the letter, but *she* could write it for him. Just as she could travel to Manticore Manor in his place and create the custom library bindings for Mr. Lightfoot's employer. How had she not seen this solution from the outset?

"A letter won't be necessary, Papa."

"We have to try, Callie."

She rose to her feet and paced along the length of the table, her mind scrambling to find arguments her father would accept. "You heard what the doctor said. Your hand needs more than a few weeks. It could be two months before you will be allowed to relinquish the plaster bandages. And after that it could take another month to regain your strength and dexterity. Begging for a few weeks is not enough. If this commission was with a longstanding, loyal client, we might be able to convince them to delay for three months. But a new client we've never worked with before? He'll turn his back on us in a heartbeat and give his business to one of the binders in Houston."

"What do you suggest we do then?" Papa's voice sounded tired. Haggard.

Taking a heartbeat to shoot a wordless prayer heavenward, Callista steeled herself for battle, then turned to face her father. "We send your highly skilled apprentice in your place."

The laudanum must have started to dull Papa's senses for his bushy brows came together in a vee of confusion. "My apprentice? I don't have an apprentice."

"Of course you do." She released her nervous grip on the sides of her white apron and held her arms away from her faded blue skirt. "Me."

Papa's eyebrows shot upward in shock before lowering into a scowl. "Absolutely not. I will not send my daughter into the home of a man I've never met. He could be a scoundrel, a wastrel, an . . . an infidel!"

Callista crossed her arms over her chest as she raised a brow. "Any other -els you want to throw into the mix? What if he's a dangerous pastel enamel spaniel?"

"This is no laughing matter, daughter." He shoved to his feet, his chair scraping the floor with a loud rasp. "I won't risk your safety."

"And I won't stand by and do nothing when I have the power to save you and our business."

Papa straightened to his full height, which was barely an inch above her own. "It's not your responsibility to save the business. It's mine."

"My name's on the door too, you know. Rosenfeld's Bindery is as much mine as it is yours." Callista softened her posture but not her stance. "I love you, Papa. More than anything on this earth. You are my family. You opened the wonders of the world to me through the pages of books, and you've trained me in a craft I'm proud to practice. But I'm not a child anymore. I'm twenty-six. An experienced businesswoman. I can do this."

Papa's shoulders slumped. "It's not your skill I question. It's your safety. If you were a man, things would be different. But you're not. Even if no physical harm touches you, there is still your reputation to consider. A woman traveling alone—"

"Then I won't travel alone. I'll find another woman on the train and adopt her as my chaperone." She breached the small distance between them and touched his shoulder. "You're always praising my cleverness. Let me do this, Papa. For both of us."

"Maybe I could go with you . . ."

Callista shook her head. "We can't afford to close the shop down for the weeks it will likely take to complete this project. It's an entire library, Papa, and from what Mr. Lightfoot describes, quite an extensive one. Someone has to stay behind to fulfill our regular orders. That was the original plan, remember? You and I are just exchanging roles."

His gaze peered deeply into hers before he gave a little shake of his head. "If I say no, you're going to do it anyway, aren't you?"

She'd never been able to hide the truth from him.

Callista shrugged as a smile twitched at the corners of her mouth. "Probably."

He cupped her upper arm with his good hand and constricted his grip enough for her to recognize that she needed to pay special attention to whatever came next.

"Promise me . . . if you feel threatened, in *any* way, that you'll come home at once. Even if it means leaving equipment and supplies behind. You're my heart, Callie. Nothing is more important to me than you."

Her heart melted at the warmth of her father's love. How she adored this man! He'd championed her in every endeavor she'd undertaken from the time she was a child. And even now, he lent his support despite his reservations, not because he wanted to save the business, but because he wanted to prove that he believed in her.

"I promise, Papa. If any trouble arises that I can't handle, I'll come home. Whether the job is finished or not."

He tugged her into a one-armed hug, and she pressed her face against his cheek as determination settled into her bones.

If trouble came, she'd find a way to handle it. Even if the manor in question truly had a fearsome manticore roaming its halls with lion claws, shark teeth, and scorpion tail, she'd not flee. Fate had bequeathed her a quest, and she'd not return until it was accomplished.

Chapter 2

Graham, Texas

"Be careful with that!" Callista stretched her arms outward as if doing so would help the groaning stagecoach driver lift the first of her two trunks out of the luggage boot at the rear of the coach.

"What've ya got in here, lady? Bricks?" The grizzled man released his grip on the trunk and huffed out a weary breath.

"No bricks, I promise." Callista smiled an apology. "Just a few book-related items."

Including an embossing press and Papa's extensive set of ornamental hand tools. All made of iron. The second trunk held the binding press and the dismantled board shear. She'd had to sweet-talk two porters at the depot in Weatherford into loading them onto a luggage cart and wheeling them from the railroad platform to the stage station this morning. The young men were exceedingly kind about helping her with the heavy trunks, but the stage driver didn't seem to share their enthusiasm.

"Yer lucky the weather held. If we'd a-gotten mired down in spring mud because of yer . . . *books* . . . I woulda kicked you off my stage and left you and your trunks for the coyotes." He shook a finger at her. "I ain't gonna risk the health of my horses for a bunch of female folderol. If you plan to return the way you came, better look into hirin' a freighter to cart your things, 'cause these trunks won't be goin' back in my stage boot anytime soon."

"Here, now, Jenkins. That's no way to talk to a lady."

Callista stifled a groan as she recognized the voice behind her.

Ambrose Batton strutted past her to clap a hand onto the stage master's shoulder. "I'll see to Miss Rosenfeld's trunks." The arrogant fellow winked at her as he stepped in to take charge.

Callista took her eyes off her trunks long enough to scan the street, hoping to find an alternative, but the pair of gray-haired ladies sitting on the bench across the way would be no help.

She did *not* wish to be beholden to the man who had been eyeing her like a wolf eyed a rabbit from the opposite side of the coach for the last six hours. She'd done her best to hide behind the book she'd packed in her travel bag, but he'd either been too dull-witted to take the hint or too full of himself to care that she desired privacy.

Thankfully, the young widow and her adolescent son who occupied the seat next to her had no such qualms about interacting with their traveling companion. The boy had been enthralled with the stories Batton told of hunting big game in Africa, India, and the mountains of Colorado. His mother went so far as to titter on a regular basis and cast flattery at the fellow like it was chicken feed. Why she'd be interested in such a rooster, Callista couldn't fathom. Sure, the man was handsome, well-dressed, and, if his stories were to be believed, well-traveled, but his ego left room for little else inside the coach.

"There's no need to exert yourself on my behalf, Mr. Batton." Callista bustled forward and grabbed one side of her trunk. "I'm accustomed to carting heavy tomes around. I'm sure Mr. Jenkins and I can manage the trunks if we work as a team."

"Don't be silly." Mr. Batton shooed her hands out of the way and grasped both ends of her trunk. "I'm happy to assist." He tugged the first trunk from the boot and then the second, setting them on end in the street. Then, with a heave so strenuous it popped the tendons in his neck into stark relief, he dragged the first one up onto his right shoulder. "Where should I deliver it?"

The strain in his voice really shouldn't delight her so much, but it did. Still, she'd hate to be responsible for him doing himself an injury, or worse, dropping and damaging her equipment, so she hurried in front of him and led him to the coaching inn's stable. "Just set them inside the barn. Here."

His elegance faded as he wrested the heavy trunk off his shoulder. Things rattled and clanked inside as he struggled to control its descent.

"Easy!"

He managed to keep it from crashing to the ground, but it still dropped with more force than she would have liked. If he had let her help instead of trying to show off by moving it himself, things would have gone much more smoothly.

Mr. Batton brushed away a lock of dark brown hair that had fallen into his face and surreptitiously swiped the perspiration from his brow as if trying to erase the evidence of his exertion. "There you go." He smiled at her with an annoying, self-congratulatory grin that made her skin itch.

"Thank you." She managed a tight little smile in return then strode back out to the street, eager to be quit of him.

Heaven save her from condescending, handsome men.

Callista's coach companion, Mrs. Dawson, pulled a fan from her reticule and employed it in a fluttery fashion as Mr. Batton pranced by to collect the second trunk while casting a wink in her direction. The young widow held her breath as if the gladiator were battling a lion instead of an inanimate piece of luggage.

"He certainly is strong, isn't he?" The question latched itself to an appreciative sigh.

It was all Callista could do not to roll her eyes at Mrs. Dawson's breathy observation. "Mmm hmm."

Strong? All right. She'd concede that point. But he was also stubborn, intrusive, and self-absorbed. If he were to march over to the stagecoach and lift it from the ground with one hand, she'd still not find him sigh-worthy.

After ensuring Mr. Batton didn't damage her second trunk, Callista left him to the admiration of Mrs. Dawson and escaped into the small staging inn. A lad of about sixteen or seventeen glanced up from a dime novel and scrambled to attention.

"Afternoon, miss," he greeted, quickly shoving his book beneath the counter. "How can I . . . ?" His eyes widened and his jaw went a bit slack as she drew near. "Um . . . I . . . uh . . ."

Callista smiled at the clerk, hoping to put him at ease. How well she remembered the first time her papa had asked her to serve walk-in customers in their bindery shop. She'd been awkward too, stumbling over her words and wishing she could hide in the back with the books.

"Good afternoon. I just arrived on the stage, and I'm hoping you can offer me some direction." She smoothed the skirt of her sage green traveling dress, hoping he didn't notice the outdated style or the frayed places on her cuffs and hem.

She'd worn her best dress, understanding the importance of making a favorable first impression on Mr. Lightfoot and his employer, but four years of wear—even if only on Sundays and special occasions—were impossible to hide. Two days of travel, first by rail then by stage, had left a fine layer of silt on the wool as well, adding to the shabby appearance.

"I'd be happy to offer whatever help y-you need, ma'am." The clerk's face reddened as he spoke, and his voice cracked a bit in the middle of his pronouncement.

Callista nodded as if she noticed nothing amiss. "You're very kind. Thank you. I have a pair of heavy trunks that I placed inside your stable. I was hoping I might be allowed to store them here until someone can fetch them for me tomorrow." She couldn't afford to pay a driver to deliver them for her. She had to trust that Mr. Lightfoot would see to their acquisition after she arrived.

The young man's head bobbed up and down with such vigor his blond hair flopped onto his forehead and covered one of his eyes. "Your belongings will be safe with us. Although . . ." He gave a quick toss of his head to send his mane back where it belonged. "I could deliver them for you. I run errands for Pa's customers all the time. Where are you staying?"

"I've been employed by Mr. Lightfoot of Manticore Manor. I understand it's a fair distance from town. Are you familiar with it? I'll need some directions if I'm to arrive before dark."

Hopefully, it wasn't farther than four or five miles. Walking wasn't ideal, but it was economically necessary. It wouldn't be so bad, though. After being crammed in a stagecoach for the past six hours, stretching her legs sounded quite inviting. Besides, she'd get to see the country and would have plenty of time to plot out the arguments she could employ to convince Mr. Lightfoot to allow her to stay and fulfill the library contract. The sun wouldn't set for another three hours, most likely. Everything would be fine.

Or maybe not. The horrified expression on the clerk's face set off a twinge of alarm in her breast.

The clerk leaned over the counter and whispered in a hushed tone. "You can't go there, miss. It's not safe. The man that owns the place is an ugly beast with a violent temper. His dog is as big as a small horse and just as mean as his master. His jaws would snap your bones like *that*!" He snapped his fingers to demonstrate.

Callista flinched slightly but managed to hold on to her composure. "I appreciate your warning. I'll be sure to keep an eye out for the dog." And pray the animal's bark was worse than his bite.

"You still think to go?" The clerk reared back, his eyebrows arched like a pair of cocked bows. "I'm not telling tales, ma'am.

I've seen the man and dog both with my own eyes. They'll eat you alive."

The local schoolchildren had likely built up an unrealistic mystique about the place, playing up the Manticore name with imaginary monsters. He'd probably been trespassing on the manor grounds when he'd caught a glimpse of someone and the excitement of the moment had flared his imagination. Boys tended to try to prove their courage in the most absurd ways. How many times had the boys in her class challenged each other to pat a longhorn on the rump without getting skewered or see who could hold their hand over a candle flame the longest?

"Well, that's a chance I'll just have to take." Callista straightened to her full height, which was still several inches shorter than that of the lanky youth in front of her. "I've accepted employment at the Manor, and I'll not renege on my promise to appear. Perhaps the dog will be chained in anticipation of my arrival." She could hope. "Now. Since you obviously know where the manor is . . ." She pulled a writing tablet from her travel bag, set it on the counter, and opened to a blank page. "Could you draw me a map of how to get there?"

He closed the pages of the tablet and pushed it back toward her. "No, ma'am. I can't in good conscience send you out there alone." He pushed back his bony shoulders and lifted his chin. "My daddy raised me to treat womenfolk with honor and to protect those who are weaker than myself. If you're set on going to Manticore Manor, I'll just have to escort you."

Considering how much he feared the place, it was quite a chivalrous offer. Her heart warmed toward the lad. "That is very kind of you, but I'm not able to pay for your time or transport. I'm happy to walk if you'll just point me in the right direction."

"I'll take you free of charge, ma'am. It's my duty as a gentleman."

Callista bit back a smile. It seemed she'd run into her own Sir Galahad. "Why don't you check with your parents? If they agree, I'll be most appreciative of your escort."

The young man's eyes lit, and a wide smile bloomed across his face. "Just have a seat for a few minutes, and I'll arrange things with my ma." He gestured to a small sitting area by the front window then disappeared through a side door.

What a sweet boy. The Lord truly had blessed her journey. She'd met Mrs. Dawson and her son at the train station in Denton and had been able to adopt them as travel companions all the way to Graham. And now the Lord had provided an escort to her destination.

Thank you.

Settling into one of the two chairs, Callista allowed herself to relax against the padded back then opened her bag to replace the writing tablet and retrieve her book. She'd covered this copy herself when Papa purchased the unbound sheets of Robert Louis Stevenson's *The Strange Case of Dr. Jekyll and Mr. Hyde* for her twenty-first birthday. She'd brought it as an example of her work, but she'd also brought it to have something that allowed her to feel close to her father. Not to mention that getting lost in a fantastical story was her favorite way to pass the time.

Swept away to London as she followed Poole and Mr. Utterson to Dr. Jekyll's residence on a hunt for truth, Callista let herself forget about foul-tempered men with terrifying dogs for a few blissful moments. Until the door next to her opened and Mr. Batton strode inside.

"Ah! Here you are, Miss Rosenfeld. I'd wondered where you'd gotten to."

Don't respond. Just ignore him. Perhaps he'll go away.

She continued staring at her book, even though she was no longer able to concentrate on the words.

Mr. Batton claimed the seat next to hers with a loud sigh. Callista grimaced. Why must he pester her so? Good manners dictated that she put down her book and acknowledge his presence, but self-preservation insisted that she keep her shield in place.

"What are you reading?" Meaty fingers clamped down over the top of her pages and yanked the book straight from her hand. He idly flipped through the pages, pretending interest. A true book lover would have turned to the title page or the spine to discover the answer to the question.

Shock at his boldness held her immobile for precious seconds. Until anger flared in her belly.

"Ah. There are those beautiful eyes. So much better to look at than this bit of leather." He aimed a flirtatious grin in her direction as if he expected her to be flattered instead of outraged by his high-handed manner.

Callista held out her palm. "My book, sir. If you please."

He raised a brow then folded the book against his chest, a teasing light entering his eyes. "And what if I don't please? What if I plan to hold it hostage until you agree to have dinner with me?"

Ugh! Could the man be any more insufferable?

"Return my book to me or I'll be forced to summon the town marshal."

Mr. Batton laughed. "The marshal? That's taking things a bit too far, don't you think, darlin'? We're just having a little fun."

There was nothing the slightest bit fun about this encounter. "Stealing another person's property is a crime. And I intend to press charges."

"Ooo wee. I didn't think it was possible for you to get any prettier, but anger suits you."

Of all the condescending, ridiculous notions!

Callista lurched to her feet, collected her bag, and held out her hand one more time. "Return my book, Mr. Batton, or I *will* summon the marshal."

"Is everything all right out here?" A woman's voice drifted from behind Callista.

Mr. Batton rose and made a show of handing her book to her over the fold of his arm as if it were some knightly favor. "Everything's fine."

Callista snatched her book and tucked it into her bag, not taking any chances.

"Miss Rosenfeld and I were just having a friendly chat. Weren't we, darlin'?"

Unable to abide standing next to the man a moment longer, Callista stormed toward the counter and the woman now standing behind it. "We shared a stage, Mr. Batton. We are not friends. And I would appreciate it if you would keep your endearments to yourself."

His smug smile finally dented. "Then I guess it's time I bid you ladies good day." His voice was tight, and his eyes shot daggers her way, but it was the challenge shining behind the daggers that made her uneasy.

He tipped his hat and exited the inn.

The moment the door closed, the proprietress giggled. "I don't think that man is used to women putting him in his place like that."

Callista released a breath. "I shouldn't have let him rile me. I apologize for causing a scene."

The woman waved her hand in dismissal. "No need to apologize to me. That was the best entertainment I've had in days." She held out her hand. "I'm Barbara Poindexter. You met my boy, Wade, a few minutes ago. He's out back hitching up the team as we speak."

"Callista Rosenfeld." She shook Mrs. Poindexter's hand, grateful for an ally. "Thank you for being so understanding. Are you sure you don't mind Wade driving me out to Manticore Manor? I'm not able to pay, and I don't want to take advantage of your family's hospitality."

"Don't give it a second thought. Though, I would take it as a personal favor if you don't ask my boy to go past the front gate. I'm not one of those who believes the tales about that place being haunted, but Wade had a run-in with the giant Mastiff that guards the grounds, and I ain't of a mind to put him in that dog's path again."

Giant Mastiff? Good heavens.

Callista swallowed rather forcibly. "You have my word."

"Thank you." Mrs. Poindexter's shoulders visibly relaxed. "I don't mean to try to scare you off when I know you're set on going, but there's something menacing about that place. No one has ever seen the owner, though his staff comes to town now and again. They never speak a word about their employer, though. It's like they're afraid of him."

"Or maybe they are just protective of his privacy." *Please let that be the reason.*

"I suppose that's possible. It just seems unnatural, is all." Mrs. Poindexter shrugged. "But I'm sure everything will be fine for you. None of his staff have ever gone missing or turned up dead."

Callista chuckled at the morbid teasing, even as her knees weakened in trepidation. She'd prepared herself to battle a hardheaded man who might think a woman unworthy of his business. What she hadn't prepared herself for was a mysterious recluse with a giant, man-eating dog, and a reputation that left the town believing the manor was haunted by some kind of ferocious beast. Perhaps she'd been too quick to dismiss Wade's account as more imagination than fact.

The door swung open behind her, and Callista spun, a small gasp escaping her. Her seizing heart relaxed when she saw Wade standing on the threshold.

"Horses are hitched and your trunks are loaded, ma'am. You ready to go?"

No, but she didn't really have a choice, did she?

With a prayer on her heart and a tight grip on the hope she'd promised her mama not to surrender, she pasted on a smile and offered her escort a nod. "Lead the way."

Chapter 3

"This is it." Wade reined in the team, tension palpable. "Manticore Manor. Or at least the front entrance."

Callista stared at the imposing wrought-iron gate. Pillars of gray stone supported black metal bars that stretched eight feet high, each one topped with an arrow-shaped point that reinforced the idea of visitors not being welcome. A fence mimicked the austere design. Black, spear-like iron rods slashing upward between unforgiving stone posts, stretching out from the sides of the gate as far as she could see in either direction.

This was the entrance to a fortress, not a home.

Her skin chilled. She told herself it was just the spring air cooling as night approached, but the resulting shivers that coursed through her limbs hinted at something more ominous. Perhaps *The Strange Case of Dr. Jekyll and Mr. Hyde* had not been the wisest literary selection for travel reading.

Was it her imagination, or were the shadows truly darker on the other side of the fence?

Wade set the wagon brake, and the click of the lever sliding into place jolted her out of her gothic musings.

"It's not too late to head back to town," he said, not for the first time. "I'm sure my ma would put you up for the night." His gaze darted to the gate, and his Adam's apple bobbed in an exaggerated swallow.

Callista pasted on a smile and manufactured some much-needed optimism. "That's sweet of you to offer, but I'm sure I'll be fine." She scooted to the edge of the bench and rose to her feet. "Come. I'll help you with the trunks."

Without waiting for his agreement, she slung the strap of her satchel over her head and arm and disembarked the wagon. Wade met her at the back of the wagon bed, and working together, they managed to drag the heavy trunks over to the gate.

Arms and back aching from the strain, Callista straightened after settling the second trunk by its counterpart at the base of the righthand pillar. Spotting a wide smudge of dust from where the trunks had rubbed against her skirt, she gave the area a vigorous brushing until satisfied no one could find her appearance amiss.

After situating her satchel to hang along her hip, she gave each of her cuffs a tug then turned to face her escort. "Thank you, again, for the ride, Wade. I'm much obliged."

"It don't feel right leaving you here, Miss Rosenfeld." He cast a nervous glance over her shoulder, probably searching for signs of the massive canine he'd tangled with on his last visit.

Gaining some level of reassurance from the fact that the lad didn't seem to find what he sought among the trees on the other side of the fence, Callista tightened her grip on her resolve. "Don't worry. Mr. Lightfoot is expecting me." Technically, he was expecting her father, but no need to split hairs.

Wade looked as if he planned to argue, so Callista did the only thing she could think of to clear his conscience. She lifted the latch, pushed the gate inward, and slid inside the opening. The bars rattled when she banged the gate closed, and the latch clanged in a way that reminded her far too much of shackles and chains.

She lifted a hand in parting. "Goodbye, Wade." Then before either of them could have second thoughts, she turned her back on the kind young man and strode down the dirt drive leading to Manticore Manor.

The path wound through gnarled trees and untamed vegetation, and every time the wind whistled through the leaves, her pulse accelerated another notch.

"'Yea, though I walk through the valley of the shadow of death, I will fear no evil: for thou art with me; thy rod and thy staff they comfort me.'" Callista murmured the words of the beloved psalm beneath her breath as she walked deeper into the unknown. Her steps slowed of their own accord as thorned mesquite trees encroached the narrowing path. Gray clouds gathered above, adding to the oppressive ambiance by casting eerie shadows and cutting her off from what little warmth emanated from a quickly sinking sun.

"'Surely goodness and mercy shall follow me all the days of my life.'"

She cast a glance behind her but saw no sign of either goodness or mercy in her wake.

Courage, Callista. Just because you can't see any evidence of his presence doesn't mean that God isn't with you. We look not at the things which are seen, but at the things which are not seen.

Even as that scriptural assurance moved through her mind, something unseen made its presence known. Something with a deep bass bark that rumbled over her like the thunder of an approaching storm.

Her head spun to the right. Her gaze scoured the shadows for the guard dog whose territory she'd invaded. She saw nothing.

Heart thumping, she rushed ahead, praying the manor would be around the next bend. But before she could reach the bend in question, the barking shifted direction, now coming from in front of her. She stumbled to a halt. Leaves rustled nearby. The low-pitched barks grew closer. Nearly upon her. She'd never be able to outrun the beast.

Callista squeezed her eyes shut, wrapped her arms around her middle, and prayed for a miracle.

Gruff barks echoed with a percussive depth so near, she could feel them like tremors in the earth. Instinct urged her to flee, but reason glued her feet to the ground. He hadn't attacked yet. She'd not give him reason to think of her as prey. Perhaps if she imitated a tree long enough, he'd grow bored and search for entertainment elsewhere.

However, the barks grew increasingly insistent. Apparently, her tree act wasn't as convincing as she'd hoped. Or perhaps she was too convincing, for the beast decided to fell her. He rammed his head into her ribcage and threw her backwards. Callista let out a startled yelp as she stumbled and landed on her backside. Eyes wide open now, she stared into the face of the massive beast who stood over her. Even her imagination could not have conjured a dog like this. On all fours, he towered over her, his fur the tawny gold of a lion, contrasting with the dark brown of his face and eyes.

He barked again, and she flinched, bringing up an arm to fend him off.

"Spartacus. Heel!"

The dog's countenance cleared as he turned toward the voice. A heartbeat later, he loped off the path and into the mesquite.

Callista scrambled to her feet, dusted off her rump, and turned in the direction the dog had gone. "Thank you, sir." She lifted her voice to be sure the man could hear her. She strained for a glimpse of him but saw nothing. "My name is—"

"I don't care what your name is. You're not welcome here." The harshness of the man's tone took her aback. "I want you off my property. Now!"

Callista fisted her hands. She had not come all this way to be bullied into leaving before she'd made it to the front door. "I have an appointment with Mr. Lightfoot."

"Mr. Lightfoot takes his orders from me, and I want you gone. End of discussion."

End of discussion? Not likely. This boorish excuse of a human being needed a lesson in manners.

Swallowing her mounting frustration, Callista called forth the conciliatory tone she used on the rare occasion she had to deal with a difficult client. "I'm sorry if there has been some miscommunication." She stepped off the path and began wending her way through the mesquite, hoping to have a civilized discussion face-to-face instead of yelling at one another across the vegetation. "I've been hired—"

"Stop right there!"

Did she detect a note of fear beneath the dominating anger? She took another step.

"Come any closer and I'll sic Spartacus on you."

She didn't believe him. He might be rude and overbearing, but he'd called off his dog earlier. Intuition told her he wasn't the type to harm an innocent woman. Scare her, yes. But not harm her.

Callista dared another step. "Please, sir. If you'll just listen to what I have to say. . ."

"I'm done listening. Be gone!"

Hurried footsteps echoed from within the brush, and a moment later Callista caught a glimpse of the back of a man clad in a reddish-brown greatcoat darting between the trees, a giant dog at his side.

He had fled from *her*. Interesting.

With the threat of the Mastiff no longer looming, renewed determination bolstered Callista's courage. She returned to the path and marched forward with purpose. The master of Manticore Manor would soon learn that she did not surrender so easily.

Why couldn't the woman just do as she was told? Everett bit back
a growl as he spied the brunette stride down the path in the wrong
direction. She'd be knocking on his front door in minutes. Cursed
female. She might be incapable of doing as instructed, but his staff
knew better than to defy his orders.

Everett reached the side of the house, braced his hand on
the railing, and launched himself over the side and onto the
wrap-around porch. He wrenched open the French doors of the
parlor and ran inside.

"Lightfoot! Timens!" His boots pounded against the polished
wood floors as he rushed into the front hall.

Timens, his dour-faced butler, met him in the entryway, his thin
mustache twitching in disapproval. "You bellowed, sir?"

"Where's Lightfoot?"

"I'm here, Griff."

Everett spun to his right, the dratted patch he wore stealing his
peripheral vision and making it frustratingly easy for his valet to
sneak up on him. Shifting his position so he could see both of
his staff at the same time, Everett gave his orders, ignoring the
throbbing in his head that signaled the onset of a migraine.

"There's a woman about to knock on that door." He jabbed a
pointed finger toward the offending portal. "She is not to be let in
under any condition. Do I make myself clear?"

"A girl?" Timens's eyes widened, a rather amazing sight, seeing
as how nothing in Everett's experience had ever shaken the man's
unflappable demeanor.

Lightfoot crossed to the narrow window that flanked the door
and inched the curtain back just enough to peek outside. "A girl,"
he confirmed. "And quite a lovely one at that."

Lovely ones were the most dangerous variety.

"Get rid of her," Everett growled.

"But, sir . . ." Lightfoot began to protest, but Everett was in no mood to listen.

He slashed his hand through the air, cutting off his valet's sentence. "Get rid of her. That's an order."

The sound of small shoes on stone steps pounded through him like railroad spikes. Everett spun away from the entrance and ran for the stairwell. He took the stairs two at a time until he reached the second-floor landing, then pressed his back against the wall and slid into the shadows.

Head throbbing, he closed his eyes and concentrated on slowing his breathing. He needed a cold compress and a dark room to sleep off the pain before knives started piercing his skull, but he couldn't rest until he was assured the woman was gone.

He'd not allow another female intent on pursuing her own agenda to destroy the peace he'd painstakingly carved out for himself over the past five years. One life had already been stolen from him. He wasn't willing to forfeit another.

Chapter 4

The knock that sounded a moment later reverberated through Everett's chest as if the stubborn woman's knuckles had rapped on his ribcage instead of his front door. He ground his molars together, bracing himself to hear her voice again.

He hadn't heard a young woman's voice in over four years. His housekeeper, Mrs. Potter, was the only female on the property, and she had to be at least fifty. He hadn't gotten a clear look at the girl on the path, but he'd heard her plenty well. Arguing. Cajoling. Yelping when Spartacus knocked her down.

The woman had backbone. He'd give her that. Standing up to a man she couldn't see was one thing, but she'd stood her ground with his dog, too. A feat most men failed to accomplish when they found their way onto his property.

The click of the latch signaled that Timens had finally gotten around to opening the door. The fellow never did anything quickly, and for once, Everett was glad. Gave him time to settle his breath so he could eavesdrop on the conversation in the entry hall directly below him.

"Yes?"

Everett bit back a grin. Timens had mastered the art of unwelcoming visitors. Disapproval fairly dripped from that single word.

"Good afternoon."

Everett winced at the feminine answer. Melodic. Educated. Completely unruffled despite the fact she'd encountered two beasts not three minutes ago.

"My name is Callista Rosenfeld of Rosenfeld's Bindery. I'm here to see Mr. Lightfoot."

Rosenfeld's Bindery? That couldn't be right. They'd contracted with a Mr. Mordecai Rosenfeld for the redressing of the library. Not a woman. *Never* a woman.

"I'm sorry, miss, but the master is not at home to guests. You may address your concerns to him via correspondence."

Good man, Timens! Everett nearly cheered aloud. Stuffy butlers might be annoying, but they had their uses. Especially when it came to sending young women packing. He could picture him easing the door closed even now.

"How fortunate that I'm not here to see your master then. Unless you consider Mr. Lightfoot your master?"

"Lightfoot?" A series of coughs and sputters ensued. "Not likely."

A chuckle filled the entry hall. "She's got you there, old chum. Let the lady in."

No! What was Lightfoot doing?

Everett banged the back of his head against the wall as a growl rumbled in his throat.

"You heard Mr. Griffin. He was quite clear about his wishes."

"I'll handle Griff. Why don't you see to some refreshments for our guest?"

She was *not* their guest. *Argh*! The pain in his head intensified tenfold. He'd obviously allowed his valet too much leniency over the years. Valet, man of business, confidant. Lightfoot wore far too many hats and was the closest thing Everett had to a friend out here. But he was still an employee. One paid to follow his instructions to the letter. Maybe he needed a reminder of who was in charge around here.

Holding a hand to his pounding head, Everett snuck a glance around the corner of the wall he'd been using as a shield. "Lightfoot." The low roar of his name filtered through the entry hall in clear warning.

Lightfoot—the blackguard—paid him no mind. The brunette's chin tipped up, however, and her eyes widened. Everett jerked back into the shadows. Foul woman, making him scurry into the dark as if he were a blasted cockroach. This was *his* house. She should be the one scurrying away, not him.

"Let's go into the parlor, Miss Rosenfeld. We can discuss our business there."

There's no business to discuss. Just evict her, already.

Lightfoot ushered Miss Rosenfeld ahead of him, then paused to glance up and shoot Everett a disapproving glare.

The dart hit his chest and punctured his conscience. Fine. He was behaving like an inhospitable cretin. He admitted it. But such was his right. His house. His staff. His rules. Until Lightfoot decided to rebel. The traitor. They'd have words later. Harsh ones. As soon as the blacksmith pummeling the anvil inside his skull took a break.

A soft murmur of voices reached him, but he couldn't make out the words as the two players disappeared into the parlor. Everett clenched his jaw. Normally he would trust Lightfoot to carry out his wishes without a qualm, but the man had no backbone when it came to females. Too chivalrous by half. If left to his own devices, he might actually offer the woman a room for the night and make Everett a prisoner in his own home.

Unacceptable!

Everett strode down the hall to the bedchamber that occupied the space directly above the parlor. He marched to the closest window, grabbed hold of the sash with both hands, and jerked it upward. Not taking a moment to consider the sanity of his actions, he ducked his head and shoulders through the opening, clasped the lip of the windowsill, then swung his legs outside. Dangling from a second story window wasn't his usual sport of choice, but he'd become a bit of a daredevil since arriving in Texas. The untamed land inspired him. Dared him to recklessness. Riding too fast. Climbing too high. Adventuring too far afield. Easy to take risks when he didn't care if he ended up in a pine box.

The patch he wore over his right eye weakened his depth perception, so it took a moment for him to line up his drop to ensure he didn't bang into the French door he'd left standing open in his hurry to beat Miss Rosenfeld to the house.

Focus, man. Everett shoved aside the pounding in his head and blinked at the objects below him until the door and railing finally settled into position. Mourning the loss of his face and the identity tied to it had been hard, but losing command of his vision had left a gaping hole in his soul. What good was an artist with only one eye?

Fairly certain he had all the obstructions mapped properly in his mind, Everett walked his hands down to the edge of the sill, then swung his body away from the door and released his grip. The balls of his feet landed with a soft thud that he doubted would carry inside the room. He smiled in predatory satisfaction and stalked closer to the open door.

". . . sorry to hear of your father's injury," Lightfoot was saying. "Nevertheless, my employer has a strict policy against having young women in his home." Perhaps the man wasn't a *complete* traitor. "I'm sure you are capable of doing the work, but as you might have ascertained, Mr. Griffin is quite adamant that you be sent away."

"I assure you that I am equally adamant about remaining."

Stubborn chit. The throbbing in Everett's head worsened.

"We have a signed agreement," she insisted, her voice polite yet firm. "You contracted Rosenfeld's Bindery to recover 250-300 books. As a partner in Rosenfeld's Bindery that agreement applies to me as well as my father. Our business underwent significant expense to purchase materials and equipment to fulfill this contract, not to mention the travel expenses incurred in getting here."

"I'm sure Mr. Griffin would be happy to reimburse your travel expenses."

If it meant getting rid of her, he'd pay for the entire job.

"But why send me away and delay Mr. Griffin's project when we have everything we need to begin right now? If he dislikes women, he can simply avoid entering the library while I'm working. I'll be no bother to him."

Why wouldn't she just accept defeat and leave? Everett balled his hands into fists and closed his eyes against the sharpening pain in his head. Throbbing gave way to stabbing.

"If he is one of those men who believes a woman's skill to be naturally inferior, I relish the opportunity to prove him wrong. I brought a sample of my work for your inspection." Her voice paused as something rustled softly.

"The embossing on this volume is exquisite," Lightfoot said with enough appreciation coloring his tone to let Everett know it was no overblown compliment. "You are obviously very talented, but Mr. Griffin intends to oversee this project personally. He's a bit of an artist himself and has a specific vision for the library. You being a woman complicates matters."

"I'm not afraid of complicated."

That was the problem. She wasn't afraid. Of anything.

He could fix that.

Callista accepted her book back from Mr. Lightfoot, praying he didn't notice the trembling of her fingers. He must see only a competent professional. Not a desperate woman on the brink of destitution. The middle-aged man's kind eyes and friendly manner had helped put her at ease during this interview, but she couldn't afford to mistake his kindness for softness. He might regret having to send her away, but he'd still do it. Unless she could convince him to speak to Mr. Griffin on her behalf, get his employer to reconsider his inflexible stance.

"I'm sure we can come up with some kind of system that would allow him to avoid personal contact with me." Though it seemed rather ridiculous for a grown man to be so allergic to feminine company he would go to outrageous lengths to avoid it. At least she wouldn't have to worry about improper advances from that quarter. "I could lay out the leather samples and tooling patterns for his inspection, perhaps sketch a few designs—"

A roar like that of a wounded bear erupted from outside the room, severing her words and stealing the air from her lungs. A man barreled through the open French doors, strode straight to where she sat and planted his feet on the rug in front of her. He towered over her, his tall, muscular frame dwarfing her in an instant, like a grizzly standing over a fawn. Golden hair hung in wild waves past his shoulders. A dark scowl twisted his mouth, made all the more terrifying by the long scar that curved from the edge of his full lips upward to disappear behind the black patch covering his right eye. Other scars littered his face as well. Slashing lines and clusters of puckered skin in varying shades of faded red and purple marred his tanned complexion. A closely-trimmed beard along his jawline probably hid even more.

"Get out of my house." The monster of a man leaned his face closer to hers as he clipped out each word in a menacing growl.

Callista's heart pounded in her chest, urging her to flee. She clutched her volume of Jekyll and Hyde to her chest as if it could shield her from his attack. Barely holding back the whimper that rose in her throat, she leaned as far away from him as her chair would allow. Slowly, her gaze shifted upward from the man's scars to his piercing eye.

The color took her by surprise. Vivid blue. Unexpected beauty in the wasteland of his rage. The lines around his eye suddenly tightened, as if he'd winced. Could pain be driving his foul temper more than anger?

"Have you lost your mind, Griff?" Mr. Lightfoot leapt from his seat, grabbed hold of Mr. Griffin's arm and pulled him a few steps backward, giving Callista some much needed breathing room. "You're scaring the poor woman half to death."

He smiled—a rather unsettling effect when combined with the predatory gleam in his eye. "She *should* be scared. It's not safe for her to be here."

Callista rose from her chair and willed her legs not to shake as she met his gaze. It was possible she'd misread that wince, but if, like Aesop's Androcles, she could find a way to remove the thorn from the lion's paw, she just might win this battle of wills.

Mr. Lightfoot's reaction made it clear his employer was acting out of character, fueling her hypothesis. He was probably used to people being frightened by his scars, especially women. Perhaps he thought to use that against her. A desperate act by a desperate man. She understood desperation. The way it drove a person to do things one wouldn't normally do. To take foolhardy risks, like standing her ground against a hostile man who had every right to have her forcibly removed from his property.

Without looking away from his face, she lowered her book and laid it on the chair she'd just vacated. She felt exposed and vulnerable without the literary shield, but only for a moment. A new strength quickly poured in to fill the void, one she recognized as coming from above, not from within. She needed no other assurance that she was on the right path.

Curving her lips into a cordial smile, she extended her hand to the man in front of her. "I'm pleased to make your official acquaintance at last, Mr. Griffin. I'm Callista Rosenfeld. Your new book binder."

Chapter 5

"What just happened?" Everett held up a hand to block the light from the setting sun as he propped the shed door open with his foot.

Lightfoot chuckled and extracted a wheeled handcart from the small outbuilding behind the house then clapped Everett on the shoulder. "You, my friend, just succumbed to a power that has been swaying men's minds since the beginning of time—the smile of a beautiful woman."

Everett frowned at his friend's assessment and shook his head in silent denial. He'd been around beautiful women before, seen their smiles, been the beneficiary of their flattery and flirtation. He'd enjoyed the attention, but he'd never been changed by it. Unlike what had happened in his parlor ten minutes ago.

The moment he'd clasped Callista Rosenfeld's hand, something had shifted inside him, like a dead limb falling from a tree. He'd felt instantly lighter yet, at the same time, concerned that he'd lost a piece of himself. A piece that had defined his identity for years.

It hadn't been her smile. Well, all right, her smile had been part of it. The woman was astoundingly beautiful, after all. Made even more so by the fact that she made no attempt whatsoever to utilize it to her advantage. No powders or cosmetics. No coy glances or coquettish wiles. Her hair had been styled in a simple knot, nothing to draw a man's attention beyond its natural thickness and rich mahogany tones. Her dress had been less than impressive. Simple lines. Unadorned style. A tad shabby around the cuffs. Utterly ordinary. Nothing enticing about it. Except that the dark green color brought out the warm tones in her sand-colored skin. And those freckles. A wide swath of them stretched from one cheek to the other, floating over the bridge of her nose. They should have detracted from her beauty. His mother had always gone into a dither if she spotted one marring her porcelain complexion. Yet on Miss Rosenfeld, they enhanced her fresh, unspoiled appearance and called to the artist in him.

Plump pink lips, finely shaped brows, well-formed cheekbones, graceful neck. Even her ears had been delicate and feminine. Yet none of that beauty had moved him.

It had been her eyes that had reached into his soul and calmed his rage. Not because of their deep brown color or their perfect symmetrical placement in her face. No, they'd touched him because they'd *seen* him. In all of his repugnant gruesomeness. And they hadn't looked away. They'd filled with neither revulsion nor pity. Instead, they'd glowed with challenge and determination, as if he were any other man who needed to be convinced of her abilities. *That's* when her smile came. While she looked him full in the face and saw only an employer—not a monster.

For a heart-stopping moment, he'd felt almost—*normal.*

"You coming, Griff?"

Everett shook off his introspection and strode forward to meet an annoyingly chipper Lightfoot who'd wheeled the cart all the way to the path while his employer pondered freckles and feminine ferocity.

"For a minute there, I thought you were going to make me fetch the lady's trunks on my own."

"I should," Everett groused. "Would serve you right for letting that woman into my house against my orders."

"Nonsense." His valet's eyes twinkled, not an ounce of repentance to be found anywhere in the man's demeanor. "You're glad she's here. Admit it."

He'd admit no such thing. The woman was going to complicate everything. Throw off his routine. Make a mess of his library. Though, he was paying her for that, so he probably shouldn't hold that against her. Still, it had taken him over a year to be comfortable enough in his own skin to cease hiding his face from his staff. Now all those insecurities were surging back to life. He clenched his jaw against the waves of inferiority and worthlessness that threatened to drag him down to the murky depths of depression that had held him prisoner for months after his injury. No! He wouldn't go back there. He'd worked too hard to climb out of that soul-shriveling pit. He'd not hide from her. If she wanted to stay, she'd just have to endure his unsightly presence. If she didn't have the stomach for it, she could leave. And good riddance.

The pounding in his head suddenly increased, reminding him that the migraine hadn't subsided, only lessened slightly. The worst of the stabbing pains had receded when their visitor shocked him out of his anger. Apparently, a release of physical tension lessened his symptoms. The doctor back in New York had indicated as much. The physician had recommended Everett remove himself from stress-inducing environments and prescribed privacy and serenity for his condition. Of course, the man had also tried to sell Everett's parents on the health benefits of an asylum he happened to own shares in, so Everett chalked him up as a profiteering quack. But maybe he hadn't been a complete charlatan.

"You know," Lightfoot said as he set the cart down near the gate, "having Miss Rosenfeld around might be good for you. Bring some freshness and light to the place and banish those dark moods that beset you so often."

"My moods are not dark." Everett grabbed the gate latch and flung it aside with enough vigor that it banged against the iron bars.

"Of course not." His valet's eyes rolled, making his opinion on the matter abundantly clear. "You're a veritable ray of sunshine."

Everett scowled as he yanked the gate open. "I'm up every day, aren't I? Bathed and groomed. Occupying my time with productive activity."

Lightfoot's gaze softened. He'd seen Everett at his worst. When despondency had its hold on him, and he'd barely been able to drag himself from bed. He'd go days without bathing, sometimes without eating as well. Lightfoot had been the one to drag his sorry carcass out of bed, to flood his room with sunlight, to scrub the stink from his sweat-stained sheets. He'd been the one to convince Everett to pick up a paintbrush again. To purchase a dog. To get out of the house and explore the world around him.

He'd spent weeks at his employer's bedside, reading aloud even when Everett had demanded to be left alone. Adventure novels mostly. *Gulliver's Travels, Twenty Thousand Leagues Under the Sea, The Adventures of Tom Sawyer, Around the World in Eighty Days*. Everett had seen through the ploy, of course. Knew Lightfoot hoped to inspire in him a thirst for life through the examples of intrepid fictional heroes. Everett had resisted, wanting nothing more than to wallow in victimized misery, but Lightfoot wore him down eventually. Though, that probably had more to do with the man's prayers than his novel reading. That and the Bible he'd left next to Everett's bed every night, the ribbon marker moved to a new underlined verse for him to find each morning.

"You've come a long way, Griff, and I praise God for it every day, but shadows still cling to you."

"I don't need a lecture, Ray. I've come to terms with who I am now. I've adjusted."

Lightfoot raised a brow. "Adjusted, huh? By naming your home after a fearsome mythological beast? You installed gargoyles on the roof corners, for pity's sake, and instead of getting a normal dog, you chose a grizzly bear."

Everett smirked. Lightfoot had never developed a fondness for Spartacus. Probably because the Mastiff had flattened him the first time they'd met, putting his paws on the valet's shoulders and toppling him into a mud puddle. "Just embracing my new identity."

Lightfoot shook his head, unimpressed by Everett's quip. "It's not a man's appearance that forms his identity, it's his character. You are more than your face, Griff. You always have been."

The stabbing returned to his head. "Tell that to my mother."

Turning his back on his valet, he strode to where the trunks were stacked and took up the first handle, waiting impatiently for Lightfoot to grasp the opposite end and refusing to meet his friend's gaze.

Everett's mother hadn't looked him in the face since the doctor removed the bandages five years ago. He could still hear her sobs. "My boy! My beautiful boy!" She'd mourned him as if he'd died. She'd avoided him as he'd convalesced, hiring nurses so she wouldn't have to see his mangled face. Father made excuses for her, claiming she blamed herself for what happened. That was why she couldn't bear to look at him. The guilt cut too deeply. Perhaps there was some truth to that, but shouldn't a mother care more about alleviating the pain of her child than seeking her own comfort? She hadn't even seen him off at the train station when he'd left to come to Texas. The most she'd sacrificed was letting her cook leave New York to become his housekeeper.

She'd written the first year. Twice. On his birthday and at Christmas. The letters had been full of chatter about what was going on in society. About an art exhibit she had visited. A few lines about his father's business. No apologies for her neglect. No mention of missing her youngest son. No promise of a visit.

Everett hadn't bothered to reply. The letters ceased after that. It seemed to suit them both to learn second-hand information through his brother. Alex at least asked how Everett was faring and looked for ways to help. He'd found a gallery in Houston willing to sell some of Everett's work and recommended a few investments that had allowed Everett to support himself instead of continuing to live off of Father's charity.

After hefting both trunks onto the handcart with Lightfoot's assistance, Everett took the lead and dragged from the front, leaving Lightfoot to push from the back. It felt good to strain his muscles, to focus on transporting physical luggage instead of contemplating baggage of an emotional sort. Miss Rosenfeld's trunks might be heavy, but they felt like feathers compared to the weight that pressed upon his spirit with crushing force whenever he thought of his family and the future that should have been his.

More than his face? Everett scoffed at Lightfoot's assessment. Maybe that held true for most men, fellows who found their worth in running a successful business or taming the land by the sweat of their brow. Everett didn't fit that mold. His value had always stemmed from his pleasing appearance and charming manner. When Lillian March destroyed the first, the second soon deteriorated to the same extreme.

He was a beast now—inside and out—and no bookish beauty, regardless of her tenacity, was going to change that.

Chapter 6

"Have another scone, dear." Mrs. Potter slid the plate of delicious biscuit-like pastries toward Callista, her grandmotherly smile promising no judgment. "You haven't tried my strawberry preserves yet, either." She scooted a small jam jar equipped with a ready spoon across the tea table. "Give yourself a good dollop and let me know if you like it better than the peach."

Callista blushed, recognizing the ploy for what it was—thinly disguised kindness. The moment the housekeeper had shown her into her personal quarters and insisted she share a spot of tea with her, Callista's stomach had growled with embarrassing ferocity. She'd not eaten since breakfast, and the porridge she'd consumed had emptied from her belly hours ago.

A practical woman at heart, Callista set aside her pride and the societal definitions of ladylike behavior and cut open a second scone. She'd need to keep up her strength if she wanted to maintain this position. Not only physically but mentally as well. Pitting herself against Mr. Griffin day after day would require a sharp wit and a firm constitution, both of which operated more efficiently on a full stomach.

Callista reached for the strawberry jam and dutifully slathered a layer onto her scone as Mrs. Potter refilled her teacup.

"Thank you." Callista looked into the older woman's sweetly round face and sensed a kinship weaving between the two of them. "Not just for the tea and treats, but for welcoming me into your domain."

She glanced around at the homey space. Tatted doilies draped each piece of furniture in the small sitting room. Red and gold roses bloomed on the papered walls, and lacy curtains framed the two windows. She couldn't imagine Mr. Griffin ever entering such a feminine space.

"Of course, my dear. As you might suppose, I get very little female companionship around here. Having you stay with us will be an absolute delight."

Curiosity burned in Callista's chest, but she swallowed her questions about Mr. Griffin's aversion to women along with a bite of jam-laden scone. She was an employee, not a guest, no matter what Mr. Griffin's staff might say. It wasn't her place to question the man's behavior or preferences. He was the master of the manor and could do whatever he pleased.

Mrs. Potter poured herself a second cup of tea as well, then winked at Callista as she stirred in a heaping teaspoon of sugar. "I'm proud of you for standing up to him the way you did. Not many people, men included, can hold their own with Everett Griffin when he's in a temper. I've got a good feeling about you, Miss Rosenfeld."

"I wish your employer shared your optimism."

"Pish posh." Mrs. Potter dismissed Callista's concern with a wave of her hand. "You're here, aren't you? Not bundled up with your trunks in Lightfoot's buggy on your way back to town. You found a way to overcome the most formidable hurdle—getting the master to let you stay. The rest should be easy. Just do what you came here to do."

Callista sipped her tea, but it did little to settle the sudden eruption of doubt in her midsection. How many clients had she served who believed her father had done all the bindery while she acted as a mere assistant? And what about the time Papa had bragged on her work, giving her full credit when Mr. Weathers came to pick up his set of bound travel journals? The customer had been waxing poetic on the fineness of the leather tooling when he'd thought Papa responsible for it. Then upon discovering *she* had been the one to wield the tools, he picked it apart, pointing out the tiniest flaws. He'd accepted the books but insisted that Papa handle his next project personally. After that, Callista had persuaded Papa not to draw any special attention to her work. Let people assume what they would. Better to satisfy the customers than drive them away by satisfying her pride.

Hiding behind Papa had never been an option with this job, so she'd convinced herself that it wouldn't matter. That her work would stand on its own merits. But that had been before she'd met Mr. Griffin and learned of the great prejudice he bore against her gender.

"You've gone awfully quiet." Mrs. Potter sought Callista's gaze. "What's troubling you?"

"I suppose I'm feeling the pressure to live up to my bold proclamations. I'm sure of my skills, but I can't control how they will be perceived."

"Especially by someone predisposed to find fault with the fairer sex." Mrs. Potter nodded as if satisfied with her deduction, then reached across the oval table to pat Callista's arm. "Don't you worry, dear. Griffin will give you a fair shake. I've known him since he was a boy, and he's always had an appreciation for artistry, no matter the gender or ethnicity of the artist. Probably because his mama is a painter and was his first teacher."

The housekeeper's voice took on a nostalgic tone. "He hasn't always been like this, you know. He used to be full of light and mischief, charming everyone he met with witty anecdotes and a ready smile."

Charming? Mr. Griffin? The roaring, inhospitable man with beastly manners and a permanent snarl? Callista prided herself on possessing a rich imagination, but she struggled to conceive such a possibility.

"He was especially popular with the ladies. Oh, how they vied for his attention! And he loved every minute of it, handsome young rogue that he was." Her expression sobered. "Until one of them turned on him." Mrs. Potter met Callista's gaze. "It was a young lady who slashed his face and damaged his eye."

Callista's chest ached as if the weight of one of her heavy trunks had just dropped upon it. Someone had done that to him . . . *deliberately*?

"Her family put it about that he had attacked her, and she had merely defended herself, but no one who actually knew the Griffins believed the story. Everett Griffin is a gentleman to his core. He might have been a bit of a rascal and a flirt, but he'd never harm a lady. You must have sensed that truth yourself, otherwise you would have fled this place moments after your arrival."

She *had* sensed it. First, when he'd called off his dog in the yard. Then again in the parlor. Even when he loomed above her, doing everything in his power to scare her witless, he'd never touched her or threatened her with anything more violent than insufferable manners and a wicked-looking scowl.

"I suppose he must have some redeeming qualities for his staff to defend him so staunchly." Callista smiled. "You and Mr. Lightfoot are both such kind souls. I can't imagine either of you remaining in the employ of someone you didn't respect."

"Timens is the same, though he hides his soft heart beneath his regimented exterior." The housekeeper chuckled softly as she leaned back in her chair. "That man *does* love his rules."

A sharp trio of knocks echoed against the wooden door.

Mrs. Potter's grin widened. "Speaking of Mr. Timens . . ." She rose from her chair but waved Callista back into her seat when she tried to rise as well. "Finish your scone, dear. I'll distract him for a few minutes by suggesting we rearrange the linen closet. That's sure to get him in a dither." Her eyes danced with merriment as she reached for the doorknob.

"I'm here to fetch Miss Rosenfeld," Timens declared in a somber tone. "Mr. Griffin awaits her in the library."

Callista finished off her scone in a single, far-too-large-to-be-ladylike bite, then washed it down with the last of her tea, determined not to keep her employer waiting despite Mrs. Potter's well-meaning schemes.

"She'll be ready in a moment. In the meantime, I had an idea about the downstairs linen closet. Don't you think it would be more efficient to move all the table linens to the left and leave the right side open for bedding?"

"No, I most certainly do not. Keeping the tablecloths and napkins on the middle shelves of *both* sides is quite essential, madam. Those are the items used most frequently and therefore should be most readily at hand. Furthermore . . ."

Callista nearly choked on her tea as she listened to Timens pontificate on proper linen organization. Goodness. How did Mrs. Potter manage to keep a straight face?

Taking a moment to rid her own expression of visible amusement, Callista brushed her hands over the waist of her dress to divest it of any crumbs that might have missed her napkin, then inhaled a deep breath and fortified herself for the meeting to come.

Be strong and of good courage. You can do this. The Lord is with you wherever you go.

Steadied and determined, Callista strode forward and smiled at Mr. Timens who faltered in his diatribe regarding the proper folding method of circular tablecloths when he caught sight of her.

"Yes, well . . . We'll continue this discussion later, Mrs. Potter. It appears Miss Rosenfeld is ready."

"I am, sir. Thank you for waiting."

"I . . . er . . . of course. This way, if you will." He pivoted and started off toward the main part of the house, his posture and stride the definition of stately.

Mrs. Potter clasped Callista's hand briefly as she passed, her eyes dancing with humor and comradery. "You'll do fine, dear," she whispered. "Just be yourself and all will be well."

Buoyed by the support of a new friend, Callista hurried her step to catch up to the butler then fell in behind him.

"Thank you for giving me a moment to finish my tea," she said, hoping to warm the butler's icy demeanor.

"Yes, well . . . should you desire tea in future, you'll need to make arrangements with Mrs. Potter to utilize her sitting room. Tea is not permitted anywhere else in the house."

"Not even the dining room?" What a strange rule. Did Mr. Griffin fear stains on his carpets or upholstery?

"Nowhere. Should you wish coffee, lemonade, or water, I'll gladly provide you with refreshment, but tea is off the menu. Master's orders. He cannot tolerate the smell of the brew."

And she'd just downed two cups of the stuff. Good heavens. What if he smelled it on her breath? She didn't need to give him *another* reason to dislike her.

"Mr. Timens?"

He must have heard the distress in her voice for he halted and turned to face her. "Yes?"

"Do you happen to have a tin of cachous I might chew? I do not wish to cause Mr. Griffin any discomfort."

The butler's stoic expression softened just a touch. "The master has never had trouble conversing with Mrs. Potter after one of her tea breaks, so I do not believe you need worry, Miss Rosenfeld. His sensitivity is not that acute."

"Oh, good." She smiled and did her best to regain her confidence, but all she could picture in her mind was greeting her employer and having him stumble back in horror as her tea-flavored breath wafted about the room like toxic gas.

A moment later, they paused outside a room in the heart of the house. The door stood ajar. "Here we are." The austere butler inspected her from head to toe, then tapped the underside of his chin with the back of his hand and straightened his shoulders.

Taking his cue, Callista adjusted her posture and raised her chin. It didn't eliminate the flutters from her stomach, but when her escort nodded in approval, a much-needed infusion of reassurance saturated her spirit.

He lifted one brow, silently asking if she was ready. Callista nodded. She knew what to expect from Mr. Griffin. He'd not catch her off-guard this time.

Timens pushed the door inward with controlled authority then stepped aside. "The library, miss. You'll find your supplies installed at the center of the room. If I can provide anything to expedite your work, you have only to ask. Mr. Griffin awaits you inside to discuss his expectations."

Feeling the oddest urge to curtsy, Callista offered a small bob of her head as she stepped past him into the room. She spotted her trunks right away but caught no glimpse of her employer at either of the tables to her left nor by the globe positioned between a pair of tall windows straight ahead. Swinging her attention to her right, her gaze stuttered to a halt as she sucked in an awe-filled breath.

Dark walnut cabinetry glistened in the dim lamplight, carved in simple elegance and stretching from floor to ceiling. Cabinet doors hid contents from waist-level to the floor, but above that stretched shelves upon shelves of glorious books. Never had she seen so extensive a personal collection. The volumes called to her like a siren, erasing all from her mind save the treasure waiting between their pages.

Her hand lifted. Her feet moved. Her eyes misted.

Heaven. Surely this must be what heaven looked like. An array of never-ending books that stretched for all eternity, filled with stories, knowledge, and experiences waiting to be shared.

Reaching the shelves, she ran a finger along the first row of spines, music erupting in her soul as surely as if she'd stroked a piano's keys. A set of library stairs in matching dark wood beckoned. She climbed one step, then another, and another, all the way to the top—craving the books on the highest shelf, the ones just out of reach. A matching set of biblical commentaries covered in rich, burgundy leather begged for her touch. She raised up onto her toes and stretched her hand above her head. Just a little farther . . .

"Those aren't the ones I've commissioned you for."

Callista recoiled at the frustrated growl and lost her footing. A yelp tore from her throat as she made a desperate grab for the top stair situated near her shins. Yet the jerking movement only worsened her balance. The tall stepladder wobbled, and in the next heartbeat, Callista plummeted toward the hardwood floor.

Chapter 7

Everett lunged forward with arms outstretched, cursing himself for being so foolish as to startle her. She crashed against his chest, her head knocking against his cheek bone with bruising force as the two of them toppled. His rear rammed the floor, quickly followed by his shoulder and the back of his head. The wind rushed out of him as one of her knees jabbed his midsection.

His delusions of chivalrous grandeur had been as flattened as his backside.

A competent gentleman would have swept the dangling damsel into his arms with grace, her arms perfectly circling his neck as he kept even her toe from striking the ground. All he'd managed to do was break her fall and amplify his headache tenfold. Some hero.

Her elbow clipped his jaw, aggravating his head. "Get off," he groused.

"I'm trying."

Good grief, man. You didn't even ask if she was hurt.

A moan pressed out of him, only partially caused by the feminine palms squishing his ribcage as she tried to rise.

"Sorry."

Cracking open his good eye, he located her waist, grabbed hold with both hands, and gently tossed her to the side. Then, gritting his teeth, he sat up slowly, careful to jostle his head as little as possible. As much as he wanted to get this initial meeting over with, he was in no condition to conduct business.

"You're dismissed, Miss Rosenfeld," he ground out.

At his words, she ceased straightening her clothes. Her eyes widened in alarm then hardened in determination. "We have a contract, sir. I admit that I allowed myself to be distracted by your collection, but you bear some responsibility for my tumble as well. If you hadn't frightened me, I never would have fallen."

"If you'd been aware of my presence, my voice wouldn't have frightened you."

Her right brow lifted in affront. "I would have been aware of your presence if you had spoken when I first entered instead of lurking in a dark corner."

"Timens told you . . . argh! Why am I arguing with you? I'm the one in charge." His voice rose to a near-roar level, which didn't help his head any. He squeezed his eye shut. "We will discuss the project in the morning. I am feeling unwell after being flattened by my resident book binder."

"In the . . . morning?" The softness of her voice cut through the pounding in his temples. "I thought you'd dismissed me."

Everett opened his eye and slowly focused on her face. "I did. You're dismissed for the rest of the night. My staff can see to your accommodat—"

Oh. She thought he'd fired her. He probably should have, but that ship had already sailed, and he wasn't one to go back on his word.

"I'm not sacking you, Miss Rosenfeld. I agreed to give you a one-week trial period, and despite what my fearsome appearance might lead you to believe, I'm a man who honors his commitments. If your skills are as proficient as you have led me to believe, you may stay until the entire project is complete. Though I pray you work quickly, for you are proving to be a plague upon my health."

He turned away, intending to quit the room before any other disaster could strike, but a featherlight touch to his shoulder blade arrested him where he stood.

"Thank you, sir." Her fingers lifted from his back but not before he felt her gratitude radiate through her hesitant touch and curl around his stone of a heart.

She'd touched him. Of her own accord. His hands trembled from the magnitude of the event, and a craving he'd thought long dead resurrected in him. A craving for affection. Tenderness.

A craving that would only lead to misery if he allowed himself to wish for what he could not have. Balling his unsteady hands into fists to hide the evidence of his weakness, he leaned away from her.

"I'll . . . do my best to be as efficient as possible," she promised.

He nodded and took a step toward the door before her voice stopped him again. Thankfully, she kept her hands to herself this time.

"Might I rearrange the tables in this room to create a suitable work area?" Her words spilled out with greater speed and enthusiasm now, as if she'd already forgotten their argument and had turned her attention to more pleasant matters. A skill he'd yet to perfect.

"Do as you see fit." She could hang from the rafters if it would get her out of his hair more quickly. "Pilfer from other rooms, if it helps."

Proud of his magnanimity, Everett stood a little straighter as he strode for the door.

"Oh, I'd hate to disturb any of the rooms currently in use," she said from behind him, her tone light and distracted. "I'll just ask Mr. Lightfoot to show me to the attic. I'm sure I can find something suitable th—"

"No!" He spun to face her, his legs braced apart and his chest heaving like a gladiator preparing to battle a lion. "The attic level is forbidden. You are not to venture above the second floor for any reason. Is that understood?"

Glossy brown eyes blinked at him from within a face so innocent she would have fooled a lesser man into believing her harmless. But Everett knew the truth. Callista Rosenfeld posed an unprecedented threat. If he failed to keep his guard up, she'd slink behind his defenses with her courage and kindness and shred all of his carefully crafted scabs, leaving his spirit more torn and bloody than his face had ever been.

Callista spent the next two hours setting up her equipment and organizing a workspace in the library. Timens and Lightfoot assisted. Timens by running through his mental inventory of every piece of furniture in the manor to uncover those best suited to her needs, and Lightfoot by actually fetching and delivering the items.

By the time Mrs. Potter called them to supper, Callista had transformed the north side of the library into a reproduction of her father's workshop. She'd rolled up the carpets and removed the finer lamps and chairs, not wanting to risk damaging the more expensive items while she worked. Then, she'd assembled the board shear and the binding press, prepared her leather-working tools and the embossing press, and set out glue pots, brushes, measuring sticks, and cutters on a large, rough-hewn table borrowed from the garden shed. Her first trunk now contained the supply of treated calfskin Mr. Griffin had ordered while the second served as storage for the gold leaf, embossing sheets, and ornamental irons that would be used for the detail work.

Callista surveyed the room, satisfaction welling inside her. It felt good to be organized. It renewed both her hope and her optimism. She had everything she needed to be successful. Her tools, her training, and her unwithering determination. All right, so maybe her determination had withered a bit after meeting the fearsome and perpetually foul-tempered Everett Griffin, but she had no doubt that a meal and a good night's rest would prove restorative. The Lord's mercies were new every morning, after all.

"If it weren't for the bookshelves, I'd think myself in the attic." Mr. Lightfoot smiled as he strolled into the room and turned a circle to take in all the changes she had wrought since his last furniture delivery. "Griff's studio looks much like this. Bare floors, rudimentary furnishings, paints and brushes readily at hand. Though his supplies are spread about much more haphazardly. He could take a few notes from your tidiness."

"You've been in the attic?" Callista's curiosity instantly spiked. "I thought the space was forbidden."

"Ah. That it is. I shouldn't have mentioned it." A flicker of guilt materialized in his gaze before melting away behind his unflappable good cheer. "Mr. Griffin allows me entrance once a month to clean and air out the space while he is engaged elsewhere."

"He must trust you a great deal."

Lightfoot's expression grew contemplative, his grin softening to a small and much more intimate smile. "He and I have been through quite a lot together. Even so, he takes care to cover all his art projects before allowing me entrance. It's not the space he guards, you see, it's his spirit. He is at his most vulnerable when he paints. As an artist yourself, I imagine you can understand his need for privacy in such moments better than most."

Actually, she didn't. She'd always worked at her father's side, the two of them supporting and encouraging each other. Then again, she didn't really consider herself an artist. An artisan, yes, but not an artist. Perhaps that was the difference. While she created beautiful designs that pleased the eye, her work didn't really touch the heart. Not like a poem or a painting or a musical composition. Still, it must be rather lonely never to reveal one's soul to another.

"Anyway," Lightfoot said with a clap of his hands and a winning smile, "enough talk about attics. Dinner is served, and I, for one, do not intend to keep Mrs. Potter waiting." He sketched a bow and offered an arm. "Shall we?"

"I'm afraid I'm not terribly presentable." She'd been so eager to get started after Mr. Griffin departed, she hadn't even taken the time to change out of her travel dress. Now she was wrinkled and rumpled and likely disheveled. She reached a hand to her hair, and sure enough, found a lock that had fallen from its pin to dangle behind her ear.

"It's just an informal supper among the servants," he assured her. "No need to get gussied up. Though, I'll be happy to direct you to the washroom if you'd like to clean the dust from your hands first."

"Yes, please." Callista couldn't have gotten gussied up if she'd wanted to, seeing as how she was wearing the best dress she owned. But clean she could manage.

After washing her hands, face, and neck, and taking a quick moment to repair her hair, Callista rejoined Mr. Lightfoot in the hall. He led her into the dining room, a large room with a gleaming mahogany table at the center, surrounded by high-backed upholstered chairs and crowned with a glittering crystal chandelier that likely cost more than the house she and Papa lived in.

"There you are, dear." Mrs. Potter scurried forward, clasped Callista's hands, and drew her deeper into the room. "I didn't know what you might like, so I emptied the cupboards and brought out a little bit of everything."

"My goodness." Callista stared in wonder at the dozens of dishes set upon the table and immediately wished her papa could share in the bounty.

"Come," Lightfoot urged as he pulled out a chair for her. "Take a seat."

At the head of the table?

He must have read the disbelief in her eyes for he chuckled. "Tonight you're our honored guest. Tomorrow, you'll be an ordinary drudge like the rest of us and can sit wherever you like."

Timens scowled as Lightfoot pushed in Callista's chair. "A drudge? Really, Lightfoot. Could you not come up with a less dreary descriptor?"

"Sorry, old friend. I made the mistake of looking in your direction while speaking, and that was the only term that sprang to mind."

Timens shot the valet a haughty glare as he assisted Mrs. Potter into her chair. "I fail to see the connection."

"Shall I fetch you a mirror?" Lightfoot pretended to head for the door, earning another scowl from the butler.

"Enough, you two." Mrs. Potter shook her head even as merriment glimmered in her eyes. She turned to Callista. "They do this quite often, I'm afraid. Pay them no mind, dear."

Callista hid a smile behind her napkin. Lightfoot must have caught a glimpse of it though, for the scoundrel winked at her, nearly causing a giggle to burst from her throat.

After the men joined the ladies at the table, the tone grew serious as Timens offered a prayer of thanks for the food. A thanks Callista felt quite keenly after the amen was spoken and platters, bowls, and other serving dishes danced by her in dizzying waves. Lightfoot seemed intent on putting some of everything on her plate. Smoked trout, bean salad, deviled eggs, red cabbage, tomato jelly, crispy toast, and some kind of gray stuff she didn't recognize. Lightfoot encouraged her to try it, ensuring her it was delicious. She followed his example, spread some on her toast, and took a hearty bite. The mineral taste of liver coated her tongue and nearly made her gag. Callista reached for her water glass, desperate to rid her mouth of the vile concoction.

Lightfoot leaned close, amusement lacing his voice. "Chicken liver paté is considered quite a delicacy back East, but it's not for everyone. Griff can't stand the stuff."

Callista dabbed her napkin against her mouth to ensure no residual paté breached her defenses. "It seems your employer and I have something in common."

"Yes, it does. I wonder what other compatibilities we'll uncover during your stay." Lightfoot leaned back in his seat and took another bite of his paté, his expression thoughtful.

Compatibilities? Odd word choice. Callista held the valet's gaze for a moment in an effort to decipher his meaning, but he only grinned and turned his attention to his fish.

He must be teasing, as he'd done with Timens earlier. She smiled even though she hadn't caught the joke and decided she must be too tired from her long day to decipher the nuances of conversational subtleties. Perhaps she'd see things more clearly in the morning.

Chapter 8

Everett rose with the sun the next morning, the anvil in his head blessedly abandoned by the blacksmith who'd plagued him so mercilessly yesterday. His stomach rumbled from missing the evening meal, but it was a small price to pay to feel human again. Dark, quiet, and the pot of coffee Lightfoot had brought up to him during one of his furniture gathering forays had helped, but it was the eleven hours of sleep that had finally put him to rights. That and the Lord's grace.

Through the years, he'd learned several tricks to still his mind while in the throes of a migraine. Unfortunately, none of them could be engaged while in the company of an interfering female. Relief required a bed, comfortable nightclothes, and closed eyes. He had to slow his breathing and focus on something other than the pain. Usually that entailed visualizing his latest painting, imagining long, smooth brush strokes, and picturing the object slowly coming to life.

Last night, however, as he painted in his mind, the solitary oak on his canvas upstairs kept being supplanted by a young woman. One with gentle curves that invited slow, smooth strokes. Large, dark eyes sparking with life and hinting at mysteries that tempted him to peer deeper. Slender chestnut brows arching with perfect symmetry upon a sun-kissed face. Youthful freckles dusting nose and cheeks like sprinkled cinnamon on golden pastry. Plump, dusky lips that curled naturally upward at the corners as if shaped by years of perpetual smiles, much like a tree bent by years of unrelenting wind.

Everett allowed the image to float through his mind anew as he washed the sleep from his eyes and dressed for the day. He'd fought against the image when it first appeared to him last night, determined to rid himself of Miss Rosenfeld's beauty and replace the vision with that of the lone oak upon a barren hill. Yet the harder he fought, the less peace he found. So, he eventually relented and allowed the artist within to recreate her perfection in his mind. Instead of the surging bitterness he'd expected to encounter at the reminder of all he'd lost, he'd thought of himself not at all. Only of her. The shape of her face and the curves of her figure. The way her eyes glistened like dark wood polished to a high shine. The contradiction between her delicacy and her strength.

He ached to paint her.

Everett shook his head at his reflection in the washstand mirror. As if she would ever sit for him. He leaned close to the mirror and examined his damaged eye. The lid had been partially paralyzed from a slicing of nerves, leaving it to droop in a lopsided manner. Then there was the opaque scar Lillian's attack left upon his cornea. It blurred his vision to a degree and made him sensitive to light, but he needed the depth perception his right eye provided when he painted, so he went without his patch in his studio. He could only manage a couple hours of work before the eye fatigued, but in those moments, he felt closest to the man he'd once been.

But then, he wasn't striving to be his old self, was he? Everett stepped away from the mirror and lifted his gaze to the ceiling.

If any man be in Christ, he is a new creature: old things are passed away; behold, all things are become new.

That verse had called his soul out of the darkness. He still recalled the way the words had leapt straight from the page to write themselves upon his heart three years ago, urging him to bury the past and leave it behind. A task he still struggled to accomplish. Bitterness, anger, and despair were not easily thrown off. He battled them each day, which was why he started each morning meditating on the verse that had brought light back into his world.

A new creature. The ironic double meaning of that descriptor appealed to the macabre sensibilities he'd developed as part of his recovery. He was definitely a new *creature*, yet it wasn't his outward appearance that Christ had redeemed, but the inner man. The vain, frivolous fellow who'd cared nothing for serious matters, including deepening his relationship with the Almighty.

For months after the attack, he'd blamed God for allowing such injustice. For failing to protect him from harm. Then he'd begun to wonder if he'd deserved such a fate. Perhaps God was punishing him as he had the haughty Nebuchadnezzar who'd credited himself for his success instead of the Lord and was driven away from people for seven years to live like a beast, eating grass and becoming wild and unkempt. A description that fell a little too close to home—living in isolation as he did, with a beastly attitude and overlong hair that made his valet groan. Thankfully, he had Mrs. Potter to ensure he didn't eat grass.

Ironic that he now took comfort from the very Bible story that had once filled him with despair. Lightfoot was to blame for that. Pounding into his head the idea that not all pain was punishment. That rain fell on the righteous and the unrighteous alike. That God could reshape broken vessels for his glory. That's how things had played out for Nebuchadnezzar. God restored his sanity and molded him into a better man in the process. Everett prayed the Lord would do the same for him. Though after yesterday's fiasco, it was clear he still had several rough edges that needed smoothing.

He reached for the eyepatch dangling by its strings from the washstand towel rack and fit it to the right side of his face. Then he grabbed the worn leather Bible from the table beside his bed, tucked it into the small shoulder bag he carried, and set out for his morning trek. On his way through the kitchen, he snagged two of the savory hand pies Mrs. Potter kept in supply under the glass dome on the counter. He chomped the first one in half with an extra-large bite, his stomach immediately growling in appreciation of the buttery pastry, savory beef, and tender potatoes that met his tongue. He wrapped a napkin around the second pie and stashed it in his bag, then let himself out through the back door. Spartacus hopped up from his haunches and wagged his tail in greeting.

Everett rubbed the dog's head with one hand as he held the rest of his breakfast out of reach. "Ready, boy?"

Spartacus let out a deep-throated *woof* then bounded ahead on the well-worn path that led to the hill of the solitary oak. About a mile away, it couldn't be seen from the house, which suited Everett. It was hard enough to bare one's soul before God. He'd rather not have witnesses for the endeavor.

The chill of the early morning air invigorated him as he trudged over hilly, broken terrain, through tall grasses, and around juniper and mesquite bushes. Familiar with the path, his mind wandered, seemingly intent on replaying images of how he'd treated the young book binder yesterday.

Abominably. That's how he'd treated her. At nearly every turn. He wished he could blame his behavior on the headache that had throbbed inside his skull, but he knew the real culprit. Fear.

Like a dog beaten and left to fend for himself, Everett had lost his trust in humanity. The destruction of his face had been bad enough, but everything that followed had turned him cynical. His mother's withdrawal. Society's eagerness to believe the March family's lies about Everett being the villain. Men he considered friends distancing themselves to protect their reputations. Every horrified look from a stranger during his trip to Texas. Each stupid kid who trespassed his property on a dare to sneak a peek at the Monster of Manticore Manor. They all hit like a kick to a mongrel's ribs, leaving him to snarl and snap even at those who didn't deserve it.

He expected to be hurt, so he avoided contact with the outside world. When the outside world dared to infringe upon his privacy, he struck out in order to reinforce the barrier he'd constructed for self-preservation. But when his usual tactics failed to send Miss Rosenfeld running yesterday, she'd left him feeling out of control. Vulnerable. So he'd snapped and growled and acted completely uncivilized.

The Lord expected better from him. *He* expected better from himself.

By the time Everett reached the tree and lowered himself to sit beneath its branches and lean against its trunk, he knew what he needed to do. But it would require a good deal of mental and spiritual fortification before he attempted something so radical.

Callista met the day with a refreshed spirit and renewed positivity. How could she not when she'd slept on a mattress that felt like a cloud? No straw pieces jabbing through the worn tick to poke her back. No rumbling snore from Papa on the other side of a paper-thin wall to wake her during the night. No cold draft whistling through the cracks to chill her nose and toes. She'd been so pleasantly cozy, she'd almost slept in.

Almost. Mr. Griffin's desire for efficiency and ridding himself of his unwanted houseguest overrode the luxury of a comfortable bed. She might have been given a chamber fit for a princess with its pale green walls, white furnishings, and plush rugs, but she wasn't a princess. She was an employee. One who still had to earn her right to be here.

Hope sees possibilities, where fear sees only barriers. Her mother's words rallied Callista's optimism as she washed her face and dressed in her blue work dress. She knew what to expect from her employer now, so he'd not surprise her again with his foul temper. He could snap and snarl as much as he liked. She'd take no offense. Neither would she respond in kind. Not as she'd done last night. Gracious. She still couldn't believe she'd argued with the man. Worse, she'd cast blame on him for a tumble that was completely of her own making. Even after he'd caught her. Or attempted to catch her. The intent to rescue had been the same regardless of his level of success, so she ought to credit him with the good deed. Yet she'd failed to demonstrate one iota of gratitude for his gallantry. She'd thanked him for not dismissing her but nothing else. How mercenary of her.

Today she would do better. She would smile and be utterly agreeable. And avoid the library ladder, no matter how strongly the beautiful books on the top shelves beckoned.

She pinned her hair into a serviceable bun and tied her work apron around her waist before striding to the door of her room. When her hand clasped the handle, she paused. *Grant me patience and a cheerful spirit, Lord. May I turn the other cheek as many times as needed and count myself blessed for having this job. May I work as if working for you, and may I bring you glory with the labor of my hands and the attitude of my heart.*

After joining Mrs. Potter, Mr. Lightfoot, and Mr. Timens in the kitchen for a simple repast of scrambled eggs, toast, and jam, Callista reported to the library promptly at eight o'clock. Not sure when Mr. Griffin might arrive to discuss his project with her since he apparently enjoyed long, rambling walks each morning, Callista busied herself by arranging some of her favorite stamp templates and ornamental tools. Imagining in her head how each finished design would look, she laid out several different possibilities for her employer to choose from, each in a different style, from very ornate to classic and reserved. Once she knew in which direction his tastes lay, she could offer individual recommendations to fit his overall aesthetic.

When she'd completed five different design options and Mr. Griffin still had not arrived, she turned her attention to his shelves. Not for personal exploration this time. She'd learned that lesson. No, she sought out books that would tell a story about their owner. Where his interests lay regarding content and what style of covers appealed to him.

The man was an artist, Lightfoot had said. He painted upstairs in a secret studio. Yet he loved books. The sheer magnitude of his collection made that assumption obvious. Some people owned large collections as a symbol of wealth or prestige. However, her new employer went out of his way to discourage visitors and sought to impress no one. His collection had been procured strictly for his own pleasure.

She perused the shelves she could reach without the aid of the ladder and found books on European architecture, Renaissance painters, and even a manual on photography. To be expected for a man interested in the visual arts. He also had tomes dedicated to topics of business, history, and religion. Although, nearly half of his collection consisted of literature.

Quite astonishing. She wouldn't have guessed him to possess the sensitive nature required to appreciate poetry, drama, or romantic novels, yet he had entire shelves dedicated to those genres. The majority of his fiction collection consisted of adventure novels and mythological tales. Finding a scholarly guide to mythological literature accidentally shelved with the novels, she slid the volume from its place and noticed considerable wear at the corners and along the spine. Curious, she flipped through the pages until a section fell open of its own accord.

What had so captured Mr. Griffin's attention that he'd propped the book open to this page often enough to cause a small break in the spine? Mystical Beasts and Mythological Monsters. Her chest ached at the telling chapter title. She thumbed through the first few pages of the section, noting an underlined passage pertaining to manticores and another regarding his namesake, the griffin.

Is this how he saw himself? As a monster? The thought sobered her even as it tugged on her sympathies. No wonder he was so foul tempered. He was fulfilling the role he'd assigned himself, a tragedy of Shakespearian proportions.

A knock brought her gaze to the door where she spied the man at the center of her thoughts. Only, he looked very little like the man she'd encountered yesterday. Probably because he wasn't scowling.

"I thought it best to alert you to my presence before speaking this time. Didn't want to risk another tumble." Mr. Griffin's mouth twitched a bit on one side, almost as if he were trying to smile.

It seemed her employer could surprise her after all.

Chapter 9

Miss Rosenfeld smiled at him. Not a new circumstance. In their brief acquaintance, she'd favored him with at least half a dozen of the things. Yet they still took him by surprise. Hit him square in the chest every time. Odd for a man who used to collect feminine smiles like a post office collected letters. In the past they'd come with such frequency and volume, he'd taken them for granted. After a five-year drought, however, he now recognized the rare and exquisite treasure of a woman's smile. Especially one as free of artifice as the one currently aimed in his direction.

"I appreciate your caution." She set the book she'd been examining on the worktable closest to the shelves then made her way toward him. Miraculously, the welcome in her gaze didn't dim as she neared. It seemed she'd acclimated to his scars faster than he'd acclimated to her smiles. "Hopefully, I'll prove less clumsy with my feet on the floor."

There was nothing the least bit clumsy about the way she moved through the room. She possessed a natural grace that many New York debutantes would envy.

Before she reached him at the doorway, she diverted to a larger worktable littered with scraps of leather, iron hand tools, and embossing stamps.

"I've laid out some preliminary design options for you to consider." Her attention moved to the table as her fingers slid along the wooden edge beneath the display. "Once I get a better feel for your personal preferences, I can tailor specific motifs for your collection."

Throat suddenly tight, Everett took a single step into the room. "Before we discuss the bindings, I need to address another matter with you."

She turned and stepped closer to him, her large brown eyes blinking innocently up at him. "All right."

"I . . . uh . . . need to apologize." The word tasted foreign on his tongue. He couldn't recall the last time his lips had shaped those particular syllables. He'd been too concerned with fortifications and barricades around his own spirit to consider anyone else's feelings. Not the most laudable conduct on his part.

Everett forced himself to hold her gaze. He had to fist his hands and lock his knees to manage the feat, but he did it. "I behaved like a boor yesterday, and I'm sorry."

Her eyes lit as if he'd just bestowed a marvelous gift, and then the blasted things began twinkling. Completely unfair of her to let them glimmer about like that. Made it hard for a man to breathe properly. Not to mention the fact that now he wanted to paint her again.

"Well, you *were* a tiny bit unfriendly when first we met, but you didn't let your dog eat me, so it wasn't all bad."

A *tiny bit* unfriendly? A rusty chuckle coughed out of him. He shut it down at once, of course, somewhat amazed his throat could still produce such a sound. "I assure you Miss Rosenfeld, Spartacus is not in the habit of eating visitors, no matter what rumors you might have heard to the contrary."

"How reassuring. Perhaps I'll take a stroll about the grounds later then." She leaned in slightly and lowered her voice. "I admit to worrying that I might be forced to pass the entirety of my stay cooped up indoors for fear of running across your hound. I usually get along quite well with animals, but your Spartacus has a rather intimidating bearing."

The thought of her being afraid of anything around his home, including himself, twisted his gut. "Have Mrs. Potter set aside some meat scraps for you," he groused. "Feed those to him, and he'll be your new best friend."

"He can be won over so easily?"

The woman had won *him* over without hardly trying, and he was far more cantankerous than his dog.

"He's seen that you're accepted at the manor, so that will help. He'll probably even try to play, which can pose a threat of a different sort. Lightfoot is still a little gun-shy around him. Spartacus's favorite game used to be Knock Over the Valet. I've trained him not to jump on people unless invited these days, though, so you shouldn't have to worry about being pounced upon."

However, Everett still sent Spartacus off to ram into old Lightfoot every now and then. Hard to resist the temptation when the result was so hilarious. Lightfoot sputtering and completely out of sorts over a bit of dirt on his sleeve or a crease in his trousers.

"In all seriousness, though," Everett continued, "I beg your pardon for my . . . unfriendliness yesterday."

Miss Rosenfeld schooled her smile into a sober line—or tried to. The disobedient edges of her mouth kept twitching upward. She dipped her head in his direction, hiding those defiant lips from him momentarily. "Pardon granted."

He dusted off the manners that had once been second nature to him and bowed to her in return. "You're very kind."

She freed her smile and it stretched wide across her face. "Oh, it's pure selfishness on my part. Holding onto an affront makes me grumpy. So much better to let it go and enjoy my day." She twirled away from him—an actual *twirl* with belled out skirt and lifted foot—and led the way back to the worktable.

Like a rat hearing the music of a pied piper, he followed, too entranced by her joy-filled demeanor to do anything else.

"My father created some custom stamps that you might be interested in utilizing. They've not yet been employed for any of our other customers, so they could be unique to your collection should you desire exclusivity."

For a price. She didn't say it aloud, but her forthright eyes communicated as much. He had no issue paying more for an exclusive design. As an artist himself, he understood how much time, thought, and talent went into crafting a motif. Should one of Rosenfeld's patterns strike his fancy, he'd gladly give the artist his due.

"Or I can fashion something based on your personal vision." She looked up from the table, admiration he couldn't possibly deserve radiating from her gaze. "Mr. Lightfoot told me of your love of painting, and Mrs. Potter mentioned that you learned from your mother years ago. I'm not a *real* artist, not like you are, but I excel at detail work. Once we establish the style and patterns you prefer, I will execute the design to your precise specifications."

"Don't sell yourself short, Miss Rosenfeld." Hearing her belittle her talents irked him far more than it should. "I've seen the sample volume you provided my man upon your arrival. You are as much an artist as I am. Perhaps more so, for your handiwork is on display in countless homes for people to see and enjoy, while most of my work is hidden away in an attic. The few pieces that have made it into galleries typically hang about for several months before some patron takes pity on them and gives them a home."

Her gaze widened as she inhaled an audible breath. "You've actually sold your paintings in galleries? Oh, how I'd love to see them."

Contaminate her natural light with his darkness? Not a chance.

Everett scowled. "They wouldn't be to your liking."

"Oh, I don't know about that." She smiled, too innocent for her own good. "I have very eclectic taste."

He bit back the sharp retort that sprang to his tongue. Snapping at her would make a hash of the fresh start they were both trying to forge. Ordering his jaw to unclench, he offered a placating smile. "Perhaps I'll paint a miniature for you as a parting gift when you leave us."

Surely he could slap some wildflowers on a card or something. Hold up his end of the bargain without letting her see inside his soul.

A tiny wrinkle appeared in her brow as she considered him, almost as if she'd been privy to the running dialog in his head. "That's a generous offer, Mr. Griffin. I'm sure my father would love to see an example of your work. We would treasure such a gift."

They would. He could see the sincerity shining in her eyes. Artist to artist.

All right. So maybe he'd take more care than just slapping some wildflowers on a card. Though, he didn't have any idea what he could paint that she would like. His style leaned into the morose, his palette muted and shadowy—none of which described the woman before him. She exuded joy and wonder, kindness and humor. Even her clothing manifested cheer. Sure, the cut of her dress was simple, the fabric plain and showing signs of wear, but it boasted the color of a summer sky. A bright blue accented with a white collar and apron, capturing the glory of the heavens when dotted with peaceful clouds. The kind of clouds children lie under and imagine to be bunnies or kittens or long-necked geese. The only color that would suit her better would be yellow—the color of the sun itself.

Good grief, man. Quit mooning over the woman and get to business. Heaven knows she's not mooning over your ugly mug.

Everett dragged his gaze away from Miss Rosenfeld's face and turned to the worktable, perusing it with far more intensity than it warranted. "Let's see what we have here."

"I set out a few options with graduating levels of ornamentation to help me get a feel for your preferences. Individual volumes can have variations on the main theme, of course, though we do recommend keeping a singular base pattern running through all the books in a particular collection."

The competent businesswoman persona she'd adopted made it easier for Everett to maintain professional boundaries than when interacting with the playful sprite who teased and smiled and admired his ability to sell paintings in an obscure gallery in Houston. Thankfully, once they dove into the actual designs, his artistic nature exerted itself, allowing him to get lost in the minutiae of hand tooling and gold embossing.

It took most of the morning to finalize his design. Miss Rosenfeld proved exceedingly adept at predicting what would please him once she grasped his preference for blending clean layouts with subtle flourishes. She even sketched a few possibilities for him, demonstrating above-average skill with a pencil. He'd taken the tablet and added his own vision to the drawing, trimming back the leafy border she'd drawn for the cover and adding stark rectangular lines that overlapped in the corners. She fine-tuned the look by inverting the corners to create a more geometrically interesting pattern and crafted a miniature version of the motif that could be utilized on the spine. They continued to fiddle, discarding and incorporating ideas until they had every detail just right.

At last, Miss Rosenfeld set aside her pencil and held up the sketch for them both to examine. "This is a beautiful design, Mr. Griffin. One that is sure to stand the test of time."

The way she drew her thumb over the edge of the sketch gave the impression she wasn't just feeding the customer what he wanted to hear. She truly admired the styling. A fact he found oddly satisfying, though why he should care about her opinion when *he* was the one who would be looking at the books for the rest of his days was beyond him. Perhaps it was simply that she was an expert in her field, and her approval validated his choices. Yet that explanation didn't ring completely true.

She laid the sketch pad upon the worktable and turned her attention to him. "Did you wish to use the dark green leather for all the new bindings, or would you prefer a variety of colors?" She pulled samples from the chest beneath the table and fanned out squares of reds, browns, and one of a deep blue. The blue called to him. Loudly.

Everett tugged the blue from the pile and laid it atop the others. "This one."

She smiled. "One of my favorites. It's more expensive, I'm afraid, but I brought enough that we could cover a small selection of books." She turned to study his shelves. "Since we are rebinding your fiction section, perhaps we could use the blue for the poetry and plays. That would leave the green for the novels, which make up the bulk of the collection." She turned back to him. "What do you think?"

He thought he would remember her in her blue dress every time he reached for Keats or Shakespeare.

"I think it's an excellent plan." He also thought he needed to get out of this library before thoughts of dresses and summer skies took his mind hostage again. To that end, he pushed back his chair and rose to his feet.

She rose as well.

"How long do you estimate this project will take?"

Miss Rosenfeld looked to the shelves that held his novels. "With the large number of books we are recovering, I would guess at least a month. Though, I could finish sooner if I worked evenings as well. I know my presence here inconveniences you."

"I'll be more inconvenienced if you wear yourself out by trying to do too much," he groused. "There'll be no working in the evenings. Sundays either. You are to take the full day off. I expect to receive your best work, and I know from experience that one cannot rush art."

Why the idea of her lengthening her visit filled him with anticipation instead of annoyance was a question he chose not to examine.

"Thank you, sir. I promise to give each book the care and time it deserves."

"Good. And since this library will be your home away from home for a while, consider it yours. You may read anything that catches your fancy during your off time." He couldn't resist adding, "Even the Bible commentaries on the top shelf."

She grinned. "I'll be sure to check the room for hidden men before I attempt the ladder again." The teasing twinkle faded from her eyes as her gaze filled with gratitude. "It's very kind of you to grant me access." Her gaze left him to scan his shelves with a longing that resonated with the book lover in him. "Choosing which to read will be a challenge. You have so many wonderful books just waiting to share their knowledge and stories."

"Yes . . . well . . . help yourself to whichever you like. Make use of the grounds as well. If this is to be your home for the next four to six weeks, you might as well be comfortable. I don't want your father to think I held you captive like some kind of prisoner."

"Oh, speaking of my father . . . might I have some paper to write to him? I'd like him to know that I arrived safely."

Everett waved toward the desk near the window. "There are writing supplies in the roll top. Help yourself to whatever you need. Lightfoot will post any letters you wish to send."

"Thank you, sir."

"Don't thank me, thank Lightfoot."

And quit calling me sir. Made him feel like an old man. What he wanted her to call him was Everett, and that realization scared him enough to prompt his escape.

"If you have all you need from me," he said as he backed toward the door, "I'll leave you to your work."

He pivoted and made a dash for the exit without waiting for a reply.

Chapter 10

May 6, 1891

Dearest Papa,

You may cease your worrying, for I am safely arrived at Manticore Manor. Mr. Griffin was initially taken aback to have a woman arrive on his doorstep when he'd been expecting a man, but with Mr. Lightfoot's support, I managed to convince him of my capabilities. He has agreed to let me stay and has provided me with a private bedchamber on the opposite side of the house from his rooms. Mrs. Potter, his housekeeper, is a diligent chaperone, and I am hopeful she will become a dear friend as well. We've already begun a ritual of sharing tea each afternoon. My employer has a strange and very strong aversion to tea, so Mrs. Potter and I enjoy a pot in the privacy of her personal sitting room. I rather like hiding away with the only other female in the house and letting down my professional guard for a time. She is wonderfully kind, and I find myself more than willing to submit to her maternal propensities.

I'm sorry that your injury prevents you from being here and seeing Mr. Griffin's library. He has a marvelous collection! The largest personal library I've ever seen. It would take your breath away, Papa. It certainly had that effect on me. Completely swept me off my feet.

Mr. Griffin truly is a book lover, not merely one who collects for the status it brings. His books are read and reread, especially the fiction titles. That is why he is having them rebound. Most of his novels have cloth covers, fitting with the current trend, but he wishes to have them redone in leather to extend their shelf life. I think you would like him, Papa. Once you get past his gruff exterior. He is an artist, like you, and has a keen eye for design. We worked together for three hours this morning to perfect the pattern I'll be using on his books. I'm so pleased with the outcome. I've included a sketch with this missive so you can picture what I'll be working on.

How is your hand healing? Are you following Dr. Haverty's instructions? Don't try to do too much too soon, Papa. As you've always taught me, doing something right requires patience and a commitment to excellence. Those values apply to healing, too. No shortcuts!

I miss you, Papa, and I pray for you every day. Mr. Griffin has been kind enough to give me evenings and Sundays off, so I'll do my best to send letters frequently to keep you apprised on my progress. Don't try to write to me with your injured hand. I don't want to be the cause of impeding your recovery. If something is urgent, you can send a telegram to the attention of Mr. Lightfoot. Otherwise, I'll assume all is well.

May God watch over you until we are together again.
With all my love,
Callista

May 8, 1891
Dear Papa,
How I missed your steadying presence beside me today. My heart pounded with such relentless force, I feared it would escape my

chest when I handed Mr. Griffin the first re-covered book for his inspection. I've presented finished products to new customers on multiple occasions, of course, but this one carried so much more significance due to the size of the contract and what it means for the future of our bindery. My knees nearly buckled from the weight of it.

Yet more than financial security played into my nerves. I cared about Mr. Griffin's reaction from a personal standpoint as well. I didn't just want his approval, I wanted his pleasure. I wanted his gaze to lighten and his mouth to curve. Having never met him, you might not understand my emotional investment, but Mr. Griffin has suffered some significant personal tragedy and does not smile easily. How I wish to change that. To give him a reason to smile every time he walks into his library and takes one of his rebound books in hand. Books are magical in that way, don't you think? Capable of eliciting joy even before one opens them. It's why the sight of an abundant library never fails to lift my spirits. But I digress . . .

He smiled, Papa! One had to look closely to catch the shift from flat to slightly less flat, but I'm counting the subtle shift as a smile, and no one can convince me otherwise. His mouth might not have curved more than a few degrees, but I could see the smile in his eye. Did I mention he only has the one? Well, I suppose he might have two, but he wears a patch over his right eye, so I can't be sure. It gives him a rather rakish, piratical air. Very fitting for a man who enjoys adventure novels. That's probably why I selected his copy of Treasure Island to recover first.

I think I held my breath through the entire inspection. It seemed to take forever for him to render a verdict, but his words have been tooled into my memory as surely as his design was tooled into the leather of that first cover.

"Excellent craftsmanship, Miss Rosenfeld."

Excellent! Not "fine" or "acceptable." Excellent. Oh, Papa, I nearly swooned from the satisfaction that flooded through me at his words. My fingers itch to get to work on the rest of his collection.

Now that I have his approval, I plan to work on multiple volumes at once. I've decided to spend tomorrow dismantling books in preparation for the week to come. I'll choose ten books similar in size and remove their existing covers. Then I'll cut new book board panels, leather, and endpapers, so they will be ready to go. I'll only be able to press two books at a time overnight in the smaller binding press I brought with me, so that will limit my pace somewhat, but I doubt I'll be able to complete more than two books working on my own, anyway. I'm not as fast as you when it comes to paring the edges of the leather, and the gold tooling will take considerable time for the more elaborate pattern chosen for the spines. While the covers are more simplistic in style, the straight lines of the rectangular design are less forgiving and will require great concentration and precision to master. Thankfully, the embossing press will make the leafy corner motifs easy to accomplish.

Since Mr. Griffin's books are relatively new, the text blocks will require little, if any, repair, which will save considerable time. I should be able to repurpose many of the headbands and tailbands as well. Mr. Griffin decided on the pale green marbled endpapers as you predicted, though he selected the gold-toned vine pattern I prefer to pair with the blue leather that we will be using for his poetry.

The size of this project threatens to overwhelm me whenever I think of the sheer number of books I will need to recover over the next four to six weeks, so I've limited myself to focusing solely on one shelf at a time. Hopefully, that will help.

I miss your hugs, Papa, and the gentle encouragement you give so generously. I'm doing my best to make you proud.

Callista

May 10, 1891
Dear Papa,
What is it about handsome men that makes them so much more hardheaded than the usual variety? Thank heavens for Mr. Lightfoot. Had he not intervened, I'm afraid I might have

done something quite shameful, such as bash the insufferable Mr. Batton over the head with my Bible. I doubt the Lord would have appreciated his holy book being used for such violence, and you know how I abhor the mistreatment of books in any fashion, but if ever there was a man who deserved to be smacked with a heavy tome, it is Ambrose Batton. Never have I met a more arrogant and aggravating man.

It all started when Mrs. Potter invited me to join her and Mr. Lightfoot in town for Sunday services this morning. I was delighted to accept, of course. Mr. Griffin prefers to worship at home. He is a believer, Papa. I've seen the Bible he carries in his satchel when he goes on his long, rambling walks each morning. The book is well worn, the pages fluffed from extensive use. However, he shies away from being around people. Do you recall the eye patch I mentioned? Well, that is only part of the picture. His face bears many scars, enough that ignorant people are often frightened upon seeing him. It saddens my heart. In truth, I barely even notice the scars anymore. His face is just … his face. But then I've never been one to care much for how a person looks. How they act is a much truer indicator of their character.

Which brings me back to Mr. Batton. I first encountered him during my initial journey to Manticore Manor. He shared the stage and filled the entire journey with tales of his hunting exploits, much to the delight of Mrs. Dawson, my traveling companion. She fed the man's ego to an alarming degree, which, now that I think about it, probably answers the question I asked at the opening of this letter. Anyway, he made himself quite the nuisance, constantly trying to engage me in conversation and even pulled a book from my hands to force my attention away from the printed page and onto him. Can you imagine such rudeness, Papa? I comforted myself with the knowledge that I need never see him again, but it seems that belief has been proven incorrect. I've since learned that Mr. Batton has leased a hunting cabin in the area. How did I learn this fascinating tidbit of information, you may ask? The man himself made it known when he tried to make off with me from the churchyard.

All right. So that might be a bit dramatic. I doubt he had any nefarious purpose in mind. In fact, he probably thought he was doing me a favor by choosing me from all the other available church women to bless with his attention. What woman wouldn't love to spend time with the handsomest man in town, after all? Me, for one. But he seemed to think I was joking when I made that particular comment. The man not only insinuated himself between me and the lady I'd been speaking to, but he had the audacity to commandeer my arm and place it within his as if we were not only well-acquainted, but courting! Then he started dragging me off toward the street, spouting some kind of nonsense about treating me to a fine lunch at the hotel. As if I would consent to dining alone with a man I barely know! A fact I would have shared with him had he possessed the courtesy to ask me to join him instead of simply assuming I'd be delighted. Thankfully, Mr. Lightfoot recognized my predicament and came to my rescue before I was forced to turn the sword of the Spirit into a cudgel of a more material nature.

I doubt Mr. Batton will continue his pursuit of me after today. Mr. Lightfoot tried his best not to cause a scene, but there were plenty of onlookers to witness the humbling moment, and the look on Mr. Batton's face made his displeasure clear. The eavesdropping crowd included a large number of unattached females, however, who were quick to offer their sympathies along with invitations to Sunday dinner. I didn't linger to discover which lady won his favor, but I'm sure the collective repaired any dents my refusal might have left in his pride.

The entire encounter made me grateful to be working for a man who appreciates the loveliness of a masterful painting or a delightfully descriptive literary phrase more than the fading beauty of a well-proportioned face.

Everett frowned at the sketch before him. The proportions were off somewhere. Perhaps he'd drawn her eyes a bit too large. They were certainly her most arresting feature, though, and deserved to be emphasized. Maybe if he added more volume to her hair . . . He swept his graphite over the page, recalling his bookbinder's glossy chestnut locks pinned up in simple, unadorned beauty that managed to capture his attention and imagination more than any elaborately curled and bejeweled coif that had floated around the society events he'd once attended.

A knock on his bedroom door jolted him from his artistic meditation and had him hurriedly flipping the pages of his large sketchbook to hide the evidence of a subject he had no right to depict.

Tugging the patch down over his injured eye, he straightened in his desk chair and turned to face the door. "Enter."

Lightfoot pushed open the portal and stepped inside, a tray of meat, cheese, and bread in his hands. "Mrs. Potter sends her regards and renews her insistence that you reconsider joining us for meals."

"A good host considers the comfort of his guests above his own convenience." Everett moved his sketchbook to make room on the corner of his desk for the food-laden tray. "I'd not want to upset Miss Rosenfeld's appetite by forcing her to behold my mangled face across the dinner table."

Lightfoot raised a brow at him and crossed his arms over his chest. "If you think Miss Rosenfeld the type of female to be put off by a few marks on a man's skin, you're a dimwit."

Taken aback by the insult, Everett rose from his chair to face his valet on equal footing. "I hardly think my courtesy deserves your scorn."

"It does when you're using it as an excuse to hide." Lightfoot sighed, then gave up his scowl and unknotted his arms. "She asks about you, you know. Worries that her presence is keeping you from your normal routines. If you really cared about her feelings, you'd quit making her feel like a trespasser and move about the house in a normal fashion. Perhaps even have a conversation with her from time to time. Two people so enamored by books are sure to find something meaningful to discuss."

Engage her in conversation? His stomach twisted. Yes, he'd survived their initial design meeting. There'd even been a few moments where he'd forgotten about his face entirely as the two of them dug into artistic details. But casual conversation was a different animal. It was . . . personal.

Everett camouflaged his unease with a scoffing sound. "I'm hardly the charmer I used to be. She'd likely find me tedious."

Lightfoot's eyebrow inched back up into the *you're a dimwit* position. "If she was interested in handsome, charming men she wouldn't have fought so hard to free herself from that buffoon who tried to make off with her this morning after church."

Something surprisingly primal surged though Everett's chest. "What buffoon?"

If some man had laid hands on her . . .

"Called himself Ambrose Batton. Visiting the area on some kind of hunting expedition. Has one of those faces women swoon over and struts around like he owns everything he sees. Tall, muscular, oozing confidence."

Everett hated him already.

"I didn't see where he came from, but I saw the flock of females hovering around him as he entered the churchyard and approached Miss Rosenfeld. The blighter had the nerve to take her arm and lead her away as if she belonged to him. I spotted her tugging to free herself from his clutches and hurried over to intervene. Batton didn't take too kindly to my interference, but too many people watched for him to take a swing at me, so we made it away unscathed."

Lightfoot chuckled. "You should have heard her scathing opinions on the man during the wagon ride home. Not once did she mention his handsome face or manly physique. She was too busy complaining about his rudeness, presumption, and arrogance." Lightfoot peered at Everett with a look that punctured his defenses. "She expressed how thankful she was to be working for a man who treated her with respect. That even when you were at your most beastly, you were twice the gentleman as Mr. Batton."

Everett had no words. His brain churned too slowly, struggling to process all that Lightfoot said.

His valet clapped a hand on his shoulder. "Your face does not define you, Griff. Your actions do. A woman of a discerning nature will see the man behind the scars. It's up to you to determine what type of man she will find when she does so."

Chapter 11

Callista turned her face to the sun and drank in the warmth, enjoying the moment outdoors before she returned to the library to continue her work. Her strolling companion nudged her in the ribs, eliciting a laugh as she stumbled sideways and tried not to topple over.

"No fair pushing me when my eyes are closed, Spartacus. I need time to brace myself for your affection." She rubbed the giant dog's fur and laid her head atop his for a quick hug.

Mr. Griffin had been right about Spartacus's loving nature. The big furball had shown no hesitation over making friends with the visiting book binder. The meat scraps Mrs. Potter provided eased the original introduction, but now the Mastiff listened for her footfalls and ran to greet her whenever she exited the house. Unless, of course, he was already occupied on one of his master's long rambles.

"Can you believe I've been here for three weeks? I'm almost halfway done with my commission." A fact that should fill her with satisfaction, not the strange emptiness that plagued her whenever she contemplated leaving this place.

The people at Manticore Manor had become a second family of sorts. Mrs. Potter with her tea parties and affectionate nature filled the motherly niche in Callista's heart that had been vacant far too long. Mr. Timens with his stuffy manners and tender heart. How she adored teasing him out of his propriety and catching him in a smile. And dear Mr. Lightfoot. Her champion and friend. She just might miss him most of all.

Well, perhaps not *most* of all.

Callista turned toward the house and peered up to the dormer windows that marked the attic where Mr. Griffin painted each afternoon. Something about the man captivated her. Perhaps she longed to soothe the woundedness inside him. Or maybe her book-loving soul simply recognized a kindred spirit. Or it could be the mystery shrouding his secret studio that tantalized her imagination. She'd never had much willpower to resist an intrigue.

He'd been less aloof of late, too. Even joined them for meals now. By far her favorite interactions with him, though, came in the late afternoons. About two weeks ago, he'd started coming to the library to read before dinner. He'd pick up the book left by his favorite chair, the overstuffed burgundy leather one with the matching ottoman, and read quietly in the corner. The only sound being the occasional turn of a page. He didn't converse with her. He *did* peek at her work as he moved past her work station—not in a critical way, just with the innate interest of an artist appreciating another's craft.

At first, his presence had been terribly distracting, but once she acclimated, she found she enjoyed having him there. It reminded her of working alongside her father and alleviated much of the loneliness that pressed in on her at the end of a day spent alone.

Four days ago, however, everything changed. He finished the book he'd been reading, the copy of *Treasure Island* that she had recovered for him, and he'd selected a new novel to read from her growing pile of completed volumes. *King Solomon's Mines.* A story only a few years old, and one she'd not yet read. He must have recognized the yearning in her voice when she mentioned that fact, for he made the most astounding offer. To read it aloud to her. As long as his reading wouldn't deter her from her work.

Too excited by the prospect of hearing the story to even contemplate turning him down, she accepted—probably with far too much enthusiasm for someone claiming to be a diligent professional.

Mercy, but that man could read. His rich, baritone voice brought Allan Quatermain to life in a way that brimmed with masculinity, perfect for an adventurer and big game hunter. And his inflections! Exquisite. Everett Griffin could have been a stage actor, so well did he capture the emotions of a scene. All without stirring from his chair. It proved quite challenging to stay on top of her work when all she wanted to do was close her eyes and listen to him.

A woman could fall in love with a voice like that.

Callista's hand froze on top of Spartacus's head. The dog whined and tilted his face toward her, as if he could feel residual frissons from the lightning that had just bolted through her. *Love?* That was *not* an appropriate notion to associate with one's employer.

Good heavens. She must banish such ridiculous romanticism at once. She was no Jane Eyre or Lucy Snowe. She was here to complete a job and save the Rosenfelds' floundering bindery. Thoughts of love and flirtation had no place in—

Crack!

Callista flinched. The sound echoed faintly, as if from a great distance, but she recognized it with ominous clarity. A gunshot.

Spartacus recognized it too, for he let out a deep *woof* then bounded away in pursuit of whoever threatened the manor. Callista raced toward the front of the house, heart pounding in dread over what she might find.

The front door flew open as she rounded the corner. A wide-eyed Timens ran from the house, calling Lightfoot's name.

That's when she saw him. Dear Mr. Lightfoot crumpled across the walkway.

No, God. Please. No.

Tears filmed her eyes as she sprinted toward him. Timens reached him first and fell to his knees beside the valet.

"Ray! Can you hear me?" Timens grabbed Lightfoot's shoulder and gently rolled him onto his back. He pressed an ear to the fallen man's chest.

A quiet groan vibrated the air.

"Thank God."

Callista's soul echoed Timens's heartfelt gratitude. Mr. Lightfoot was alive!

Coming alongside, she looked to the butler for direction. "How can I help?"

Timens reared back as if he'd been completely oblivious to her presence. Then, just as quickly, he narrowed his eyes. "Get in the house, woman! There's a shooter about."

"Surely he's gone by now. There've been no more—"

"I'm taking no chances. In the house. Now!"

Callista ignored his directive, more concerned with aiding Mr. Lightfoot than preserving her personal safety. "But I can help." She crouched down and slid a hand beneath his right shoulder. "You can't carry him inside on your own."

Timens batted her hand away, a sure signal of the seriousness of his distress. "If you want to help, fetch Mr. Griffin."

Mr. Griffin. Yes. He'd want to know about his friend. Armed with a task to complete, Callista forfeited the argument and ran for the house.

Hiking up her skirt, she sped up the stairs. She didn't hesitate for even a heartbeat when she reached the forbidden attic steps, but she did call out Mr. Griffin's name to give him notice of what was about to happen. Apparently, it wasn't notice enough, however, for when she threw open the door and stumbled inside, she found him paintbrush in hand and missing his eye patch.

The sight of him with both eyes staring at her in horror slowed her just long enough for a familiar thundercloud to fall over his stunned face. A thundercloud they didn't have time to indulge. Before he could rage at her, she dodged forward, grabbed the hand without the paintbrush, and started dragging him toward the door.

"Yell at me later. Mr. Lightfoot's been shot."

Her dumping a bucket of water over his head would have shocked Everett less.

"What?"

His mortified anger vanished in an instant as all self-focused thoughts fled. *Lightfoot shot? How? By whom? Where?*

A thousand questions bounced around in his brain as he dropped his brush and stumbled after Miss Rosenfeld, but the largest rose to the surface.

"Is he . . .?"

"Alive." She paused at the doorway, the anguish she'd hidden beneath her air of command finally breaking through. Her voice cracked. "Mr. Timens wouldn't let me stay. I have no idea how bad it is. Please, hurry. Timens will need your help to bring him inside."

Her distress amplified the fearful ache in his own chest and stirred the ill-timed desire to take her in his arms and whisper words of comfort. Instead, he briefly cupped her arm and met her watery gaze. "I'll see to him," he vowed.

Then he turned and charged down two flights of stairs, her voice ringing out behind him with instructions to head to the front door.

By the time he reached Timens's side, Lightfoot was conscious and arguing with the butler about being able to walk. Never had he been so happy to hear the two of them bickering.

"Stubborn-headed dandy. You can't even sit up on your own, I'm not about to let you try walking."

"Well, if you'd quit . . . " A groan interrupted. ". . . torturing me by pressing handkerchiefs into my wound for two seconds and help me sit up, maybe I could get . . . out of the dirt."

"I'm rendering aid, you fool." More concern than heat colored the butler's response.

"What you're doing . . . is getting blood . . . all over my favorite jacket."

Everett dropped to his knees beside Lightfoot, angling his head away from the sunlight as pain shot through his right eye.

He bent over his friend, not liking the ashen pallor of his valet's complexion but smiling anyway.

"Stop worrying about your clothes, you peacock, and let us carry you into the house."

Lightfoot shifted his gaze to Everett's face and grimaced. "Ah, Griff. The strangest thing happened. A bullet somehow found its way into my arm."

"So I see."

Everett slid his arm behind Lightfoot's back as he shared a look with Timens, who did the same.

"What do you say we take a closer look at that inside?"

Lightfoot moaned as Everett and Timens lifted him into a sitting position. Once up, his face paled even further, and he almost passed out. He gritted his teeth, though, and managed to hold on to consciousness.

"I think," he gasped. "I need a minute . . . before we move again."

"I can carry you," Everett offered, but Lightfoot waved him off.

"Not in front of the women," he whispered. "Don't want to . . . scare them."

Timens made a scoffing sound. "Too late for that, old boy."

For a barely conscious fellow with a hole in his arm, the heat of Lightfoot's glare was impressive. "All the more reason to give a show of strength. To reassure them." He turned to Everett. "My legs still work. Just got to get my head to cease swimming."

Timens caught Everett's eye. "He took a pretty good knock to the back of the skull when he went down."

"Help me get him up. I can walk him in while you ride into Graham to fetch the doctor."

Timens nodded and together, they pulled Lightfoot to his feet without too much jostling. Everett stretched his friend's uninjured arm over his shoulders and wrapped an arm around his waist to hold him upright.

Everett took on the majority of Lightfoot's weight then released Timens to his fetching duties with a nod. After the butler scurried toward the carriage house, Everett tilted his head toward his valet. "Ready?"

"Not really, but it beats returning to the dirt."

Everett grunted as he dragged his friend toward the house. Lightfoot managed to help him for the first ten feet or so before he began to slump, growing heavier with every step. Worried the valet might have lost consciousness, Everett jostled him slightly when they reached the bottom of the porch steps.

"You know," he said between clenched teeth, "this would be a good time for you to start living up to your name."

A weak but decidedly lucid chuckle exhaled from the man at his side. "Sorry, Griff. It's . . . the extra lead. Makes me . . . heavy."

The weight dragging on Everett's body might not have lessened, but the weight on his heart did. If Ray could joke about the situation, it couldn't be too dire.

At that moment, Miss Rosenfeld ran down the steps, arms outstretched. "Let me help you."

"Don't touch his arm," Everett warned.

She halted, obviously at a loss as to how to help without touching him.

"The desk chair in my office," Everett ground out as he leaned to the left, using his few inches of greater height to lift Lightfoot's feet from the ground. "Has wheels. Bring it."

She whirled and dashed back into the house, leaving Everett to scale the steps without an audience. The woman was quick, though, arriving back with the chair before he cleared the last step. She wheeled the chair into position at the top of the stairs and held it steady while Everett lowered Lightfoot into the seat.

"Mrs. Potter said to bring him into the kitchen." Miss Rosenfeld led the way into the house as if ready to clear the path should an obstacle jump from a closet to block their path. "She has water boiling and the medicine box prepared."

Everett pushed Lightfoot down the hall, careful not to move too fast and run over the man's no-longer-light feet. When they reached the kitchen, Mrs. Potter took over like an army general. She immediately took scissors to Lightfoot's shirt, earning a more distressed moan for her disregard of fine tailoring than any complaint related to his actual wound. Everett looked up and shared a grin with Miss Rosenfeld, taking comfort from the relief he saw mirrored in her eyes. She seemed to share his assessment. Lightfoot would be fine.

The deep reverberations of Spartacus's barking drew Everett to the back door. Miss Rosenfeld followed.

"He took off the moment we heard the shot," she said, placing her hand high on his back as she tried to peer over his shoulder. "He might have found the shooter."

The feel of her hand made him ache to close his eyes and savor the rare treasure of a woman's touch, but her words had his jaw tightening.

The shooter could simply be an inept hunter whose shot had missed its intended target, but Everett's gut rejected that theory. They'd never had hunters in this area before. And who would be foolish enough to aim *toward* a person's home? It's not like they couldn't see it. It was the largest house in the county, for crying out loud. Could've been kids taking a potshot at the Monster of Manticore Manor. Everett's stomach cramped at the thought of Lightfoot taking a bullet meant for him. If kids were to blame, they'd likely be too scared to cover their tracks. If he could trail them home, they'd get to see the monster up close when he knocked on their door and had words with their parents.

And if it hadn't been kids?

Everett frowned. If someone was targeting his home, his staff, he needed to know. He took a step backward and reached for the rifle kept on a rack above the kitchen door.

"Wait," a quiet voice said near his ear.

He turned and found her pulling a string from her apron pocket.

"I grabbed this from upstairs. In case you had need of it." She opened her hand to reveal his eye patch.

Two truths pounded in his head with the force of a migraine. One, she'd been looking at his half-dead eye all this time and had not been repulsed enough to turn away from the sight. Two, he'd left his patch looped over the easel supporting his current painting. If she'd found the patch, she'd seen his artwork as well. The one piece he never wanted her to see. The unfinished portrait of a sweetly beautiful book binder.

Another bark from Spartacus shook him from his humiliating ruminations. With a mechanical movement he accepted the patch from her hand. He moved too slowly, though, for she clasped his arm before he could make an escape.

Her earnest eyes found his without a single flinch. "Be careful."

Careful? He'd left careful behind the moment he'd let Callista Rosenfeld into his house. And it seemed he'd soon be paying the price for his reckless folly.

Chapter 12

Everett hunkered down next to an area of flattened prairie grass about five hundred yards northwest of the manor. His jaw clenched as he recognized the pattern. He'd seen it before. When he and Alex had attended shooting competitions at the Creedmoor Rifle Range on Long Island. The thick rectangle where the prone shooter's body pressed into the earth. The two off-set circles where his elbows rested as he aimed his rifle for a long-distance shot.

The bullet that took Lightfoot down hadn't come from a reckless kid or an incompetent sportsman. It had come from a sharpshooter. Which meant the shot had been deliberate and targeted. Targeted at whom, though? Lightfoot or him?

Everett stood and squinted across the distance to the manor. He could make out the front door, but with his poor depth perception, he struggled to bring it into focus. He and Lightfoot were of similar height and size. Lightfoot was perhaps more slender and definitely better dressed, but could someone differentiate those details from so far away?

The question ate at him all the way home.

After praising Spartacus for his good work in chasing off their invader, Everett stepped through the back door and into the kitchen. He glanced around the room, taking stock of who was there.

"I shooed Miss Rosenfeld back to the library."

Apparently, a hole in the arm hadn't hampered Lightfoot's ability to discern Everett's thoughts.

"After letting her spoil me a little first."

Sitting at the table nearby while she snapped string beans into a pot, Mrs. Potter huffed out a breath full of skepticism. "A little? That girl fetched you a pile of pillows, a footstool, and a clean pair of trousers then sat at your side and mopped your brow while you just sat there drinking in all the attention."

"Well, I *am* injured, you know." He glanced pointedly at his bandaged arm. "And as much as I adore your starchy bedside manner, Mrs. Potter, Miss Rosenfeld is a tad more solicitous."

"The girl's too young to know better."

And too kind to change even if she did learn such a lesson, Everett thought.

Mrs. Potter set aside her pot and rose to her feet. "Now that Mr. Griffin's returned, I'll let him assist you into the trousers you wanted so badly." She wiped her hands on her apron and walked the long way around the table so she could come alongside Everett and whisper a warning. "He's putting up a good front, but he's weak and in a lot of pain."

Everett nodded, noting the strain lines around Lightfoot's mouth and the pallor of his skin. "I'll be gentle with him."

"I hear you whispering over there, you know."

Everett flicked away the grumbling accusation with a wave of his hand. "We're swapping recipes. Nothing to concern you."

"Uh huh. And I'm the king of England."

"Congratulations on your promotion." Everett set his rifle against the wall and strode to where his friend sat in a regular kitchen chair near the wall, pillows behind his back and head and one beneath his right arm. Both feet were propped on the library ottoman. A glass of water sat on the ledge of a nearby cupboard to Lightfoot's left, within easy reach. Not a bad throne, all things considered.

He lowered himself into the vacant chair next to Lightfoot, the place Miss Rosenfeld had likely occupied prior to his return. He took care not to lean back and rumple the pair of perfectly pressed trousers hanging over the chair back.

"Embarrassed to see the doctor in dusty trousers, are you?"

"A gentleman must uphold his standards."

A gentleman must also wait for a lady to leave the room before discussing darker matters. A notion both men adhered to as they waited for Mrs. Potter to cross the threshold and tug the kitchen door closed behind her.

"What did you find?" Lightfoot asked in a low voice the moment the housekeeper left.

"Not much," Everett hedged. "Whoever the shooter was, he didn't stick around to be discovered."

"But you found something." Lightfoot jabbed him with a pointed stare. His valet had an uncanny ability to sense when Everett was holding back. A rather obnoxious skill when one was trying to protect his friend from worry. "Spit it out, Griff. A man can't solve a problem by hiding from it."

Another obnoxious skill was his ability to spout irrefutable wisdom at the drop of a hat. Everett exhaled a beleaguered breath. "Spartacus led me to a patch of flattened grass. Gave the impression of a man shooting from a prone position. One who had likely lain there quite a while, judging by the matted nature of the grass."

Lightfoot frowned. "So, someone targeted me?"

"He could have thought you were me. We are similar in build." Everett shrugged, trying to minimize the chilling thought. "I'm sure there's more than one person who wouldn't mind ridding the area of the local monster."

"You know my feelings regarding that term," Lightfoot scolded.

"Yes, well, your opinion fails to match the majority of our neighbors."

"You could change that, you know. If you let them get to know you."

Everett swallowed the growl rising in his throat. "Now's not the time to rehash that old argument. Someone is taking shots at the people under my roof, and we need to figure out who."

Lightfoot nodded. "And why." His brows suddenly arched high on his forehead. "You don't think . . .? No, surely not. No one's that petty."

Everett leaned forward. "What?"

Lightfoot shifted in his chair and winced. "That fellow who was bothering Miss Rosenfeld a couple weeks ago. What was his name . . . Patton, maybe? No, Batton. Ambrose Batton. Remember? I told you how she complained about him. She said something about meeting him on the stagecoach. He'd tried to impress her with tales of his hunting exploits. The last two Sundays, I've made a point not to leave her side after services. It's possible he views me as some kind of impediment to his courtship. He could have followed us home last Sunday, made note of our location. Returned later to eliminate the man standing between him and Miss Rosenfeld." He shook his head, disregarding his theory. "I'm letting my imagination get away from me. This sounds like the plot to some gothic novel. No rational man would shoot another just to gain access to a woman who's already made it clear she doesn't desire his company. Especially with so many other women vying for his favor."

"I'd wager Miss Rosenfeld's beauty could rival Helen of Troy, and we know how irrational men became over her." Everett rubbed the side of his face where scarred, puckered skin abraded his fingertips. "We can't rule out a twisted mind just because the man carries himself normally in front of others, either. I made that mistake once before. I'll not make it again."

Especially if the man was after Callista.

Callista. He'd not allowed himself to think of her in such familiar terms before. She was an employee, after all. But she was also a woman under his protection, an artistic colleague, and—dare he consider it—a friend. He looked forward to the afternoons they spent together in the library, seeing her smile, hearing her hum softly while she worked, and watching her eyes light with satisfaction and appreciation each time she pulled a finished volume from the book press.

"It might be best for all of us to stick close to the manor for a while," Everett said. "Especially you and Miss Rosenfeld."

Lightfoot glanced down at his bandaged arm. "I doubt I'll be up to the task of driving to town anytime soon, but it might be wise to warn our guest. She's gotten to where she enjoys a nice stroll about the yard each afternoon." His eyes took on a fierce light. "We've all grown quite fond of the dear girl and would be devastated if any harm befell her."

They weren't the only ones. For the first time in half a decade, Everett was finally becoming comfortable in his own skin. His mangled, disfigured skin. And all because a woman whose spirit was even more beautiful than her breathtaking face saw *him* instead of his scars. She'd given him back a piece of himself he'd thought never to reclaim, and in the process, stolen his heart. Not that he would ever admit to such a thing. As kindhearted as she was, he couldn't expect her to love a beast.

Everett stood and clapped his hands together. "I guess we better get you in these clean trousers, then, so I can go have a chat with my book binder."

Callista worked her paring knife outward along the margins of the leather she had cut for the next book in the collection. The edges of the leather had to be thinned where they would fold over the boards to reduce their bulk and create a smooth surface once the endpapers were pasted in. Usually, she found the rhythmic scraping of the knife soothing, but not today. Not with Mr. Lightfoot nursing an injury from a gunshot that could have killed him.

Thank you for sparing his life, Lord. Grant him healing and ease his pain.

"Miss Rosenfeld?"

She jerked slightly at the sound of her name, the razor-sharp blade digging into the leather a little too deeply. Glancing up, she spied Mr. Griffin walking toward her, and she immediately set her blade aside and rose to meet him.

"How's Mr. Lightfoot?"

Mr. Griffin offered one of his half smiles, the kind that proved Mrs. Potter correct in calling him a charmer. "Much better now that he's wearing a fresh pair of trousers. I swear that man cares more for his clothes than the skin they were designed to protect."

Relieved at the news, Callista offered a smile of her own. "I'm thankful he feels well enough to fuss over his clothes. When I first spotted him on the ground, I feared the worst." She rubbed her arms, the chill returning to her bones as she recalled that heart-stopping moment.

"I did, too." Mr. Griffin gestured for her to accompany him to the settee positioned near the chair where he liked to read. "In light of what happened, I think we need to discuss some things. If that is all right with you?"

"Of course."

She moved to the small sofa and sat down, surprised when he sat beside her instead of in his chair. The moment he sat, the warmth emanating from him wrapped around her like a blanket on a cold night. His nearness offered the comfort she hadn't known she'd been craving. She twisted inward to see him better, her knees accidentally brushing against his. As a gentleman would, he immediately shifted to remove his legs from touching hers. The urge to chase him and resume the contact surprised her with its strength, but her comfort wasn't worth his *dis*comfort, so she refrained from violating the small buffer separating them.

"The shooter was gone by the time Spartacus led me to his location, so we don't know who he was or what his motive might be for firing upon the manor. However, I'm fairly certain that the shot was not an accident."

Someone was targeting the good people of Manticore Manor? How dreadful! A fire lit in Callista's belly, one flaming with the need to protect the people she cared about. Straightening her posture like a soldier reporting for duty, she looked Mr. Griffin in the eye. "What can I do to help?"

His brow arched. "What can you do . . .?" He wagged his head, that half smile making another appearance. "I thought this discussion would frighten you. I should have known better. You're not one to back away from trouble. I saw that for myself the day you arrived."

"Nothing is more important to me than family, Mr. Griffin, and while you might find me terribly sentimental, I'm not ashamed to say that I've come to think of all of you here as a second family. You've opened your home to me, treated me with kindness and respect, and practically adopted me as one of your own. I've come to care about all of you a great deal, and I'll do whatever I can to help."

He stared at her without blinking. Then, after a nerve-wracking set of heartbeats, his lashes closed over his magnificent blue eye and raised again as if clearing away his shock.

Had her talk of family really been so extraordinary? She'd noticed definite familial tones in the way he interacted with his staff, especially Mr. Lightfoot. But then, he'd been with them for years. He'd only known her for a few weeks. Perhaps he found her statement presumptuous.

"I've overstepped, haven't I?" She hung her head. "I do tend to lead with my heart, I'm afraid. I apologize for making you uncomfortable."

"Don't apologize." His voice rumbled with raw ferocity. "Please." He softened his tone as she lifted her head. "You've done nothing wrong. In fact, you've given me a great gift. There are very few people in this world who have treated me with the kind of loyalty and honor you've just demonstrated. Your comments merely took me by surprise. That's all."

Callista smiled as relief coursed through her. "I'm glad I didn't cause offense."

"Not at all. I assure you."

"Good." She raised her chin and gave him her best ready-for-action nod. "Now. What can I do to help?"

His expression turned serious. "Until we know that it is safe, I would prefer that you not spend any time outdoors."

"Will *you* be spending time outdoors?"

He leaned back, his brow arching. "Yes, but I'll be armed."

Callista fought not to roll her eyes. "If you think carrying a weapon will prevent a bullet from ripping through you, you're less intelligent than I gave you credit for."

That expressive eyebrow of his slashed downward in a tight line. "I am responsible for the safety of the people in this household. Including you. I will not cower inside these walls and wait to be attacked a second time."

"No, you'll just go out there and make yourself an easy target." Callista pushed to her feet, too upset at the idea of him being struck down to sit in comfort. "Don't you see that the people of this house care about you? You speak of protecting us, but who will protect *you*?"

"I suppose I'll have to depend on the Lord for that." He'd risen from the sofa the moment she had, and now stood barely a foot from her. So close, she swore she could feel him breathe.

"God doesn't always protect those we love," she murmured, her voice cracking as she remembered her mother.

"I used to blame him for not protecting me, too. The day . . . this . . . happened." He gestured to his face, and Callista's heart throbbed in her chest. He'd never discussed his scars openly with her. "But as time passed, and the freshness of the betrayal faded, I began to see that God *had* protected me, just not in the way I expected. He'd spared my life, yes, but he'd also spared me from a lifetime of misery being married to a woman incapable of love. And if I'm completely honest, he protected me from my own arrogance and pride."

Callista couldn't look away from him. He was opening himself to her, and she couldn't bear the idea of that door closing again. So she gave a gentle push to the invisible boundary between them, and delved into personal territory. "That's what the rose represents, isn't it?"

She'd caught a glimpse of a couple of his paintings when she'd fetched him from the attic, but the rose . . . the rose had arrested her.

He nodded slowly. No anger evident on his face.

Dare she ask? She longed to learn more of his heart, to see it reflected in his art. To share that piece of him that he kept locked away. Grasping a surge of impulsive courage, she found her voice. "Would you show me someday?"

His throat worked up and down as his gaze locked on hers. She saw the struggle reflected in his gaze, ingrained caution battling a burgeoning trust.

Let me in, she silently pleaded.

Chapter 13

"The doctor's here, Mr. Griffin." Mrs. Potter's breathless announcement from the library doorway saved Everett from having to give an answer.

He followed his housekeeper from the room, leaving Callista behind with nothing more substantial than a murmured apology. Her image, however, clung to his mind with the same tenacity as buffalo burs clung to Spartacus's fur. Especially those expressive eyes of hers. Their dark fathoms had peered into him as if she saw his soul, and for some inexplicable reason, she acted as if she wanted to see more. And, heaven help him, he wanted to show her. To experience a level of human connection that had been closed to him for years. Lightfoot had seen his art, but they'd never discussed it. Probably because the one time Lightfoot had asked about a painting, Everett had snapped at him, his emotions too raw back then to put into words.

Yet, in the few minutes Callista had been in his studio, she'd discerned his struggle. The pain, the loss, and the search for hope.

He'd seen it in her expression. Heard it in her voice. What amazed him even more, though, was the fact that she didn't ask him about her portrait. She could have accused him of using her image without permission and been perfectly justified in doing so. She could have coyly preened about being his muse. She could have simply assuaged her curiosity by asking about it. Heaven knew, if he'd found a likeness of himself in someone's studio, he would have noticed little else. But not Callista. She'd noticed the rose.

The Last Petal Falls. He'd completed the painting two years ago and should have sent it to the gallery by now. It was one of his better pieces and would likely fetch a good price. Yet he hadn't been able to part with it. Each of his paintings carried a piece of his soul, but that one . . . that one still had a grip on him. Just as that final petal hung suspended for all time in the painting, unable to fall, he couldn't escape the feeling that something held him back as well. A pain he wasn't quite ready to lay down. A pain that pricked anew when the doctor met him in the entry hall and drew up short at the sight of Everett's face.

The man recovered more quickly than most, probably due to his exposure to all manner of grotesque injuries, but the reaction still stung.

More concerned about Lightfoot's healing than his own at the moment, though, Everett pretended he hadn't noticed the doctor's startlement and offered his hand.

"Thank you for coming."

The man shook his hand with a reassuring firmness and peered at him through a pair of round spectacles. "Glad to help. Where's my patient?"

Mrs. Potter stepped forward. "If you'll follow me, sir? Mr. Lightfoot is in the kitchen."

Everett brought up the rear, happy to let his housekeeper take the lead. He remained in the background as the doctor conducted his examination, only stepping in when the physician needed assistance moving Lightfoot from the chair to the table. Mrs.

Potter created a pillow from some folded towels, and Everett did his best to keep Lightfoot talking while his friend faced the indignity of being sprawled upon a table like a half-dressed Christmas goose.

After the doctor poked and prodded, his examination turning Lightfoot quite pale, he reached for a bottle of ether and poured a liberal amount into a handkerchief.

"We're going to put you to sleep now, so I can dig out that bullet and sew you up. All right?"

Lightfoot clenched his jaw and offered a nod, but a second later, he grabbed Everett's arm with his good hand, his eyes wide with something Everett thought never to see—fear.

"You'll stay with me?"

Everett nodded, his throat clogging as memories surged of all the times Lightfoot had stayed with him. By his bedside in his darkest hours, a beacon of hope that things *would* get better.

"Every moment, my friend."

Lightfoot nodded and laid his head back to accept the ether. Thankfully, the doctor worked quickly and with skilled precision. Within an hour, he had removed the bullet, cleaned and stitched the wound, and bandaged Lightfoot's shoulder. Everett and Timens worked together to carefully carry the valet to his room, so he could rest in a bed instead of the unforgiving kitchen table.

The doctor followed and gave some final instructions. "He's not to exert himself for at least three weeks." He handed Everett several packets of medicinal powders. "Add these to his tea or water to help with the pain. When he feels strong enough to be out of bed, he will need to wear a sling for additional protection and support. It's good for him to exercise the fingers and hand of his injured arm, but the shoulder itself should be kept as immobile as possible during the early stages of healing. In the meantime, watch him for signs of infection, and fetch me right away if the wound putrefies."

"Thank you, doctor." Everett shook the man's hand again. "We'll keep a close eye on him." He glanced at the bed where Lightfoot dozed. He'd awakened from the ether when the men had carried him to his room, but the medicine had left him groggy. Everett figured some rest would do him good. He collected the chair from the desk in Lightfoot's room and moved it to the side of the bed. Everett had made a promise, and he intended to stay by his valet's side until he awakened fully.

Timens, having regained his usual aplomb after seeing that Lightfoot would indeed recover, gestured for the doctor to precede him into the hall. "I'll see you out, sir."

The doctor raised a brow. "I'll make you a deal, Mr. Timens. I'll see myself to my horse if you see to that giant hound of yours. Had your housekeeper not been watching for my arrival and called the hound to heel, I doubt I would have made it to the front door."

"If Timens is with you, Spartacus will leave you alone," Everett said.

"In that case, I'll gladly accept your escort, Mr. Timens."

The butler nodded, and the two men exited the bedchamber. Timens closed the door behind them.

Everett settled into the wooden desk chair then opened the top drawer of the bedside table and pulled out the Bible he knew he'd find there. He opened the cover, intending to flip through the pages to find one of Lightfoot's favorite passages, but an unfamiliar, feminine handwriting on the presentation page captured his attention.

To Ray Lightfoot, on the occasion of our marriage, February 4, 1871.

You wooed not only my heart, but my soul as you demonstrated God's unconditional, steadfast love. Because of you, I know what it is to be loved by an eternal God. And because of God, I know what it is to be loved by you. Thank you for being my light in the darkness, Ray. I am forever yours.

Babette.

Lightfoot had been married? Everett had never heard the man speak of a wife. What had happened to her? Stomach twisting, he turned to the page where family deaths were recorded. Expecting to see one name, Everett's heart bled when he found two.

Barbara Renee Lightfoot, August 12, 1873, taken in childbirth, age 21.

Lucas Aaron Lightfoot, August 12, 1873, stillborn.

Everett's eyes misted and his chest felt as if it had been placed inside Callista's book press. The weight of the unexpected sorrow stole his breath.

"I see you've unearthed my secrets."

Everett lifted his face to find Lightfoot's heavy-lidded gaze on the Bible in his lap.

"I didn't mean to pry. I thought to read . . ." What he'd thought to do didn't really matter now, did it? Everett closed the Bible, but he couldn't close his heart to what he'd learned. "I'm sorry, Ray. So very sorry."

The words felt completely inadequate, but he had nothing better to offer.

"It was a long time ago. Before I came to work for your family." His voice carried the haze of the lingering effects of the ether, but his face didn't register sorrow. Instead, he actually smiled. It was the last thing Everett expected to see from a man contemplating his dead wife.

"Ah, Griff. You would have liked Babette. She was full of sass, but so quick to laugh." Lightfoot's gaze moved to the ceiling as if watching memories of his beloved traipse by. "I still remember the day I came to work as a footman at the estate where she served as a maid. She was so vivacious and beautiful. I was instantly smitten." A chuckle vibrated through his chest. "And I did a terrible job of hiding that fact. One time she caught me staring at her when I was supposed to be moving furniture for her to clean beneath. She wiggled her feather duster over my face, and set me to sneezing like an ill-mannered youth. 'If you have something to say to me, Mr. Lightfoot,' she said, 'use your mouth, not your eyes.' So I did. Told her how I thought she was the most beautiful woman I had ever seen and that I'd love to take her to dinner on our half-day off. I'll never forget her response. 'Ask me again when you know me well enough to admire something more than what you can see on the surface.' Ah. That woman led me on a merry chase. And even knowing what I do now about how little time we would have together, I'd not change a thing."

Lightfoot twisted his neck to face Everett again. "Love with the right woman is worth the cost, Griff. Worth sacrificing a man's pride, his autonomy, and even his security. Those things are a pittance compared to the riches that come from sharing your heart with a woman who loves you as fiercely as you love her."

"Why are you telling me this?" Everett shifted in his chair, trying to banish the vision of Callista that had materialized in his mind at the mention of women and love.

Lightfoot smiled. "Because you need to hear it." His expression grew serious. "I would have passed on the same wisdom to my son, had he lived . . . and grown to be as hardheaded as you."

Everett grinned at the teasing, his chest tightening to think that Lightfoot thought of him, at some level, like a son. Even if barely a dozen years separated them in age.

"God presented you with a gift when he sent Miss Rosenfeld to bind your books. All of us can see it. Mrs. Potter, Timens. Shoot, even that ridiculous dog of yours recognizes how special she is. I think you see it too. You're just too afraid of being hurt to do anything about it."

Lightfoot slid his arm from beneath the covers and opened his palm. Sensing what he wanted, Everett placed the man's Bible in his hand. His chest tightened when Lightfoot's fingers curled over the spine and he closed his eyes as if he could still feel his wife's touch in the leather.

Gradually, he opened his eyes again and pinned Everett with a look that carried a heartrending mix of hope and grief. "Don't waste time on fear, Griff. Time's the one thing you can never get back."

Lightfoot closed his eyes and rolled his head to a more comfortable position on the pillow. He pulled the Bible onto his chest and clutched it near his heart as he drifted back to sleep.

Everett blew out a quiet breath as he leaned backward in his chair. His head ached from all the new information that had exploded in his mind over the last several minutes. Ray . . . married. And a father. In all the time he'd known him, he'd never guessed. Of course, he'd never asked, either. Lightfoot had been hired to serve a self-absorbed youth who only cared about his valet's knowledge of fashion so he could impress his friends and whichever ladies happened to be about. Why the man had volunteered to stay with him after his injury, Everett couldn't fathom. Or maybe he could. The man lived his faith. And through that living, influenced the lives around him. His wife's inscription testified to that truth, as did Everett's experience. Ray cared about people at the soul level.

Everett ran his fingers through his hair, grabbing a handful at the crown of his head and tugging against his scalp until it hurt. He would have been lost without Lightfoot. Without Mrs. Potter and Timens. He'd done nothing to deserve their loyalty, their kindness, yet they'd given it freely. Leaving their homes to move to the wilds of Texas. Putting up with his foul moods and his inhospitable nature.

If they weren't a living, breathing demonstration of God's grace, he didn't know what was. And yet God had brought him another gift. At least according to Lightfoot. One he desperately wanted to accept despite his complete unworthiness.

A tremor ran through Everett's chest. He'd never wooed a woman without his looks to rely upon. He wasn't even sure how to go about it.

Admire something more than what you can see on the surface.

Babette's words rose to the surface of his mind. Spoken by a beautiful woman who wanted to be appreciated for more than her outward appearance. Hadn't he secretly longed for the same, even before his injury? To be appreciated for his art or his literary knowledge or just for himself alone? He'd mourned the loss of his face so deeply because, at some level, he'd believed it was the only thing that had given him value. Thankfully, with Lightfoot's help, he'd started to find his worth in being a child of God. Chosen and beloved by a Father who looks not at the outward appearance but at the heart.

Perhaps it was time to stop hiding his heart behind the thorny hedge of his pain, and expose it to view. Callista had already provided the invitation when she asked him to show her his paintings. All he had to do was crack open his chest, and let her in.

Chapter 14

Callista had done more praying than book binding over the last two hours. Praying for Mr. Lightfoot, the doctor, and even Mr. Griffin. Distracted by her concern for Mr. Lightfoot, she hadn't trusted herself to tool any of the leather, so she'd cut book board instead. The simple task required less concentration, but she'd still managed to mismeasure a couple of the pieces. She'd trim the boards down later to use on smaller volumes, so it was no great tragedy, but it still irked her inner perfectionist.

Thankfully, Mrs. Potter stopped by the library to update her on Mr. Lightfoot's condition after the doctor left, assuring her that all was well and that he was expected to make a full recovery. The good news cheered her heart, but it failed to clear her mind. In fact, it worsened her distraction. For without her friend's injury to worry over, her mind turned to a different injured gentleman. One whose wounds stretched beneath the surface and couldn't be tended by the local physician.

Callista sighed as she released the bladed arm of the board shear, then wiped her moist palms across the front of her apron. She needed to quit thinking about her employer in such intimate terms. She'd been hired to bind books, not to bind the hidden wounds of a man far above her station. Yet hadn't God called his people to do good unto all men, especially unto them who are of the household of faith? If she could help Mr. Griffin find peace in his circumstances, shouldn't she seek ways to do so?

God also called his people not to think of themselves more highly than they ought, and it could very well be her pride that made her think she had the power to help him. Or perhaps selfishness—seeking an excuse to deepen their interactions.

She couldn't deny that she was drawn to Everett Griffin. And not just in a pure-hearted, altruistic way. Her heart leapt each time he entered the library. Her gaze sought his at the dinner table. She didn't simply listen to him when he spoke, she hung on his words, caring far more about his thoughts and opinions than her position warranted. She longed to impress him with her artistry and to be the one who made him smile. She wanted him to desire her company the way she desired his.

Because she was developing feelings for the man.

And wasn't that the height of foolishness?

She'd only be at Manticore Manor for another three weeks, four at most. If by some miracle Mr. Griffin *did* come to view her with some affection, that wouldn't change the facts. When she completed the final book cover, she would return to her father and assist him at the shop. Mr. Griffin would remain here, taking rambling walks with Spartacus and hiding from a world who recoiled from his scars. Even if he chose to give up his reclusive habits, his parents would never approve of him marrying a woman like her. Poor, outspoken, and completely ignorant of societal rules and expectations.

Yet, their growing friendship need not lead to something romantic. Callista straightened her shoulders and did her best to ignore the sharp pang of disappointment the realization wrought. Her future might not align with his, but she still longed for him to have the most joyful future possible. One filled with friends and family, where the cobwebs of old pains and regret had been swept clean. She was rather handy with a broom. Perhaps she could help rid his soul of some of those cobwebs before she left. The assurance of his happiness would make her own easier to grasp.

Having sorted things out, Callista refocused on the project at hand and lined up a new piece of book board atop the base of the shear and raised the bladed arm to make the straight edge cut.

"Miss Rosenfeld?"

Callista's hand froze midair as she sucked in a quiet breath. It really was quite unfair of him to barge his way into her attention again when she'd just worked so hard to push him into the background. Yet, the predictable leap of her heart at the sound of his voice made it clear that all the logic and planning in the world wouldn't curb her pleasure at being in his presence.

Determined to conduct herself in a professional—and definitely *not* besotted—manner, she steadied her hand and finished her cut before turning to face him.

"Yes?"

Her gaze unerringly found the vivid blue of the eye not hidden by the patch. His eye really was the most extraordinary color. Almost turquoise. Yet the color wasn't what had her pulse picking up speed, it was the vulnerability glowing from its depths. She'd seen kindness, concern, embarrassment, and plenty of anger. But she'd never seen him nervous. It tugged on her heart in a way that had her moving toward him with hand outstretched before she even realized she'd taken a step.

"What is it? Has Mr. Lightfoot—"

"No. Ray is fine. He's resting. I just . . ." He rubbed the back of his neck with his hand and dropped his gaze to the floor. "You asked me a question before the doctor arrived, and I didn't give you an answer." He lifted his chin and shyly met her gaze.

Callista's heart pounded so hard, she longed for a chair back or table to steady herself. With none in her immediate vicinity, she settled for widening her stance slightly and hoping her knees held.

Her question had been far too personal. She'd realized that about five minutes after he'd left the library. She should retract it. Keep a proper distance between them. But her heart wouldn't let her. She longed to know this man. Deeply and personally. Not simply to feed the attraction she felt toward him, but because she sensed that if he opened the door to her, it would be easier for him to open the door to others. It would give him freedom to face the world as himself and not a man cloaked in mystery and scandal.

So instead of hiding behind her own wall of safe propriety, she took her courage in hand and opened the gate, praying he wouldn't close it in her face.

"Do you have an answer for me now?"

"I . . . ah . . . There's about an hour left of good light . . . If you're still interested . . . I could show you some of my paintings."

Yes! She managed to keep the gleeful cry in her head and away from her tongue as she responded with more decorum.

"I would like that very much."

He smiled, and her heart flipped with the wild abandon of windblown book pages.

He offered her his arm as she imagined a gentleman would do for a lady at a ball or when taking a stroll through a manicured garden. She slid her fingers into the crook of his elbow, her breathing growing slightly ragged at the contact. It didn't help matters that she felt a shiver course through him as well when her hand slid over his sleeve. Hearing Mrs. Potter talk, Callista expected her employer to be quite accustomed to escorting women about, yet he reacted to her touch as if it were an entirely new experience—one that left him as shaken as it did her. The observation did nothing to strengthen her knees as she departed the library on his arm.

When they reached the stairs, he stepped aside and gestured for her to ascend ahead of him. Strange that she should miss the feel of his arm so keenly after such a brief connection, yet it seemed she'd acquired a craving for his touch. A rather imprudent development, to be sure, but one she found little motivation to dismantle.

At the third-floor landing, Callista pressed her back toward the wall so that Mr. Griffin could take the lead in entering the studio. This was a sacred space, and she wanted to honor his gift by taking nothing for granted.

His hand trembled slightly as he turned the knob, but the door opened, and they both stepped inside.

Large windows lined three sides of the studio, flooding the oversized room with late afternoon light. The tangy smells of paint and turpentine tickled her nose, and her shoe heels echoed loudly against the wooden floorboards. A worktable of sorts stood in the center of the room, covered with paint tubes, small jars of pigment powder, a variety of brushes, and an assortment of palettes bearing smears of colors. A stained smock draped over one corner of the table near a crate of what appeared to be blank canvases stretched over wooden frames.

Her companion said nothing as she walked deeper into the room, so she continued her exploration in silence. Four easels formed a U shape in front of the back wall. Her gaze shied away from the one at the front right. She'd glimpsed it the last time she'd been in this room and was too embarrassed to give more than a fleeting perusal. The one behind it proved much more welcoming. The rose. Fragile yet beautiful. Intricate details. So lifelike, she could practically feel the softness of the scattered petals against her skin. She wanted to study it more closely, but a stronger impulse drew her away. The lure of the yet unexplored paintings on the other side of the studio. Leaving the rose with a silent vow to return soon, Callista veered to the left.

The first canvas was unfinished, the bottom third untouched save for thin, charcoal markings sketching out what looked to be a hillside. A single tree stood atop the hill. An oak. Tall and sturdy, though its limbs were gnarled and scarred. At first, she marveled at the intricate details of the leaves and the bark and the shading of a sunset in progress in the sky behind the branches. However, when she shifted her attention from the individual brush strokes to the picture as a whole, a heaviness settled over her heart. The dark color palette emphasized the shadows cast by the setting sun, but something else panged within her breast. It took a moment for her to figure out what it was, but when she did, her eyes grew misty. The tree stood alone. Strong and proud in isolation.

She felt him watching her, could sense his apprehension as she examined his work. It took great courage for an artist to reveal an unfinished, imperfect project. She owed him the same gift of vulnerability, so she turned to him and let him see the rawness of her reaction. He stood a few paces behind her and to the right, and her chest ached at the vision he presented. The solitary oak, strong and proud but alone.

No more.

She stretched out her arm to him, her hand open. He hesitated then slowly clasped her hand. She smiled and drew him near, determined to banish his loneliness, at least for the short time they had together. Neither of them said a word, but palms pressed together in silent communion as they moved to the second painting.

Another tree. Only this one was not alone. Several others circled behind it in the background, their details blurred and indistinct in contrast to the lifelike starkness of the tree in the foreground. She didn't recognize the genus. Perhaps an elm? What she did recognize was the jagged bolt of lightning slashing through a dark, stormy sky to spear the tree like a fiery javelin. The bolt split the trunk in two, leaving it charred, broken, and hollow. Raw pain emanated from the brush strokes, but the hollowness depicted hurt her heart the most. It must have been one of the first pieces he'd painted after his injury. She squeezed his hand tight as a tear slid down her cheek. She wiped away the moisture as she moved to the painting of the rose.

He'd chosen such a dark palette of colors. Muted browns, reds, and greens filled the foreground. A single, faded rose stood in a vase atop a small table situated near a window. The flower had turned its face toward the sun, but not even the light had been able to halt its withering. Fallen petals formed a lopsided pile in front of the slender vase. The stem drooped, its neck bowed as if beneath an invisible weight. One petal remained attached, its edges browned and wrinkled, a mere shadow of its former glory. Yet a beam of sunshine poured through the window, bathing the flower in light. Welcome warmth banished the shadows of death and sorrow, infusing the image with hope. He hadn't given the viewer a glimpse of what lay beyond the window, but Callista imagined a beautiful garden filled with rose bushes in bloom. Roses ready to bring cheer and sweet perfume to the shadowed nook.

She thought to bypass the final painting, her cheeks heating as she recalled the subject matter on that particular canvas. However, Mr. Griffin resisted when she tried to cross to the small table and chairs at the back of the room. He tugged on her hand and drew her to stand before the unfinished portrait of the woman she saw in the mirror every day.

"Do you see what is missing in this one?"

His quiet murmur rumbled through her, stirring enough interest to overcome the awkwardness of viewing herself through his eyes.

"Missing?" She peered at the portrait, not looking at the face pictured there but at the overall design.

There *was* something different about this painting. It dawned on her slowly, like the sun pushing past the horizon in early morning. Pinks, whites, and cheerful yellows had replaced the shadowy hues of the other paintings. Instead of brokenness and grief and isolation, this painting spoke of joy and light. The woman in the painting smiled, her eyes alight with laughter. In truth, it was so different from the others that, had it not been housed in the same studio, she would not have guessed that the same artist composed them all.

"Pain," she whispered. "I don't see your pain."

Chapter 15

A tremor coursed through Everett at the emotion in Callista's voice. The connection of her hand in his caused his soul to swell to the extent that his skin felt as if it must stretch to accommodate the growth. He still couldn't quite believe she'd voluntarily taken his hand. He knew it had been an act of compassion. It carried no romantic meaning. Yet now that the link had been forged, he doubted his ability to sever it.

"I don't *feel* the pain when I look at you."

Her lashes dipped over her eyes, and the pink in her cheeks darkened. Drat. He'd embarrassed her.

"I shouldn't have painted your likeness without permission. If you wish, you can take it with you today. Slice it to ribbons, hide it away in one of your trunks, set it afire."

Though, any of those would be a travesty.

"Gracious!" She craned her neck so that she could face him. "I could never destroy a piece of art in such a manner. Even if you did take liberties and paint me in too flattering a manner."

"Too flattering?" A surprised laugh coughed out of him. "My feeble efforts fall far short of doing you justice, Callista."

The moment her given name slipped from his lips, he froze. He'd crossed a line, one that couldn't be uncrossed. One that left him dangling from a high limb, his hand outstretched to her, with no guarantee that she wouldn't hack off the branch and send him careening to a bruising collision with reality.

She blinked like a startled doe for a moment, then ever so slowly, that shy smile of hers reappeared to play havoc with his stomach. "I like conversing with you as if we're friends. I'd like to think it's not far from the truth. Rather like you and Mr. Lightfoot."

Good grief. He hoped not. His feelings for Callista bore little likeness to his friendship with Lightfoot. Yet he understood what she meant. Friendship, or any type of intimacy, between an employer and his employee created a natural imbalance in the relationship. Mutual respect and trust had to take precedence over the bounds of employment for the relationship to work. A trust he needed to be careful not to abuse.

"I do consider us friends, Miss Rosenfeld. Though, I apologize for using your given name without permission. I seem to be taking several liberties of late, don't I?" He gave his head a small shake in self-abasement. "Having you here in my studio, gazing upon my paintings, created an atmosphere of intimacy that made me forget myself. Please forgive me if I have made you uncomfortable."

Compassion lit her eyes, but something else sparked there too. Pleasure, perhaps? He hoped so. He really didn't want her pity.

She squeezed his hand, then brought her other palm around to cup his fingers from the outside as well. His heart banged against his breastbone.

"There's nothing to forgive." Her smile unknotted his gut. "To be honest, I *liked* hearing my name. I've never been away from my father for such a length of time, and I miss the easy banter we always share. And if you truly do consider us friends, then I see no harm in disposing with formality when we are in more intimate circumstances."

"In that case, you must call me Everett as well."

Her lashes lowered. "Everett."

A tremor spread through him when she spoke his name, and he had to resist the urge to draw her into a true embrace. His feelings had raced past friendship in a blink of an eye and dived straight into something dangerously deeper.

"About the painting . . ." She turned to face the portrait once again, her hand finally slipping free of his.

"Consider it yours," he blurted. "Whatever you wish me to do with it, I shall."

Though, he really hoped she wouldn't vote for destroying it. He'd not experienced joy in the act of painting since before his accident. Catharsis, yes, but not joy. Not until he'd started painting her. Yet, even if she asked him to set the portrait aflame, he'd not hesitate. She'd awakened the joy of creation within him, and he'd not despise her gift with his own selfishness.

"You mentioned possibly painting a miniature for me to take home to my father. Would you consider finishing this painting and allowing me to gift it to him? He and I have birthdays only a few days apart, and we always celebrate them together by exchanging handmade gifts." A mischievous gleam entered her eyes, making it clear that some level of competitiveness was involved with this tradition. "We're not allowed to spend any money, so creativity is our currency. I'd thought to hand tool him a hat band from a scrap of blue leather left over from your binding project. Papa's always loved the color blue. But I like the idea of presenting him with this even better." One of her fingers cautiously touched the edge of the canvas, as if she feared marring the artwork. "It's technically handmade. Just not by me. And since you are giving it to me, no rules would be violated regarding the financial restrictions. He'll be so surprised!"

Her delight was palpable, and it fueled his own. So unlike his experience with birthdays in his past, days filled with expensive gifts and tepid enjoyment. His favorite foods graced the table, yet he'd always been eager to quit the obligatory family dinner and head to the club with his friends. Back in New York, he would have scoffed at the idea of handmade gifts. But when Callista spoke of them, they suddenly seemed like the most valuable commodity on the planet. Because of the love and thoughtfulness woven into the very fabric of the offerings.

"How soon is your father's birthday?"

"Next week, actually. But we made plans to celebrate after I finish the job, so there's no rush."

Next week? Which meant *her* birthday was also next week. He needed to talk to Mrs. Potter. Make plans. Handmade gifts. And maybe something extra . . . something to help him finish her portrait.

Who knew that sitting still could be so taxing? Callista wrinkled her nose, wanting to scratch the itchy spot on the left side but not wanting to disturb whatever vision Everett had prepared. He'd worked so hard to position her head just so, trying to match the face on the canvas. When he'd shown her his studio two days ago, something had shifted between the two of them. Up here, they were no longer employer and employee. They were friends. Perhaps *more* than friends.

Heat rose to her cheeks as she recalled the feel of his gentle fingers positioning her chin at the desired angle and encouraging her to relax her shoulders. All traces of the beast she'd met the first day of her arrival had vanished. Yes, his scars were still there, but his demeanor had completely changed. He spoke in cultured tones, his voice never raised. He sought her gaze instead of avoiding it, and when he touched her, there was such tenderness in the contact that she felt as if she were a priceless treasure being treated with utmost care.

A soft masculine chuckle broke into her thoughts. "You can scratch if you need to. I won't lose my place."

She immediately took him up on the offer, groaning softly in satisfaction as her fingernail rubbed away the irritation.

"Shoulders," he said, amusement lacing his tone.

"Sorry." She'd sagged a little at the relief of being able to scratch and now hurried to reset her posture.

Never would she have guessed that she would have cause to sit for a portrait. Such activities were reserved for the wealthy, not ordinary girls in worn-out clothes who bound books for a living. Yet Everett had cajoled her into agreeing, insisting that it would help him finish the portrait in a timelier fashion if he could use her as a model for an hour a day. So here she was, sitting in the light of an attic window while a man painted her likeness. The situation should make her feel terribly self-conscious, and it did at some level, knowing his artist's eye surely spotted all her imperfections. Yet he found ways to put her at ease while giving her a chance to observe him as he worked. A privilege few enjoyed, and one she'd not squander.

Trust had sprouted between them and was growing at a remarkable rate. Spending her midday breaks with him allowed them not only to work on the portrait but to talk. They discussed favorite books and artistic interests, but they also spoke of families. Yesterday, she'd told him about her mother and how she still felt her loss, and he'd spoken of his. Of how her reaction to his injury had cut him deeply even as he acknowledged that he still missed her—missed the closeness they'd once shared. Artist to artist, and mother to son. Callista had urged him to write to her, to take the first step toward mending the rift. To forgive her for being weak and forgive himself for being harsh. He'd promised to think about it, and she'd promised to pray—for him and for his mother.

As she watched him paint, his forehead lined in concentration, his gaze moving from her to the canvas, her heart stirred at the visual evidence of his trust. His eye patch hung off the edge of the easel. He'd tried to keep it on yesterday but had quickly grown frustrated by his lack of depth perception and had asked her permission to remove it. He'd apologized, going on about how unsightly it was and how he would understand if she found it too off-putting. Of course, she'd already seen him without it once, and while it made her ache for the pain he'd suffered, it was simply part of him and caused her no distress to see it. He'd still tried to hide his injured eye from her at first, keeping the right side of his face strategically behind the canvas or pulling his long, tawny hair forward like camouflage. Yet today, he moved with greater ease, almost as if forgetting about his eye entirely. Such trust was a gift, and she vowed he would never regret extending it to her.

"You can relax now." Everett stood back from the canvas and tilted his head as he examined his work with a critical eye. "I think I've finally got your hair right."

Callista rose from her chair, rolled her shoulders and stretched the stiffness out of her neck that had accumulated while she'd dutifully imitated a statue. "May I see your progress?"

He shrugged. "If you like. Just remember, much of the shading and detail work will come with the final layers."

As she came around to his side of the canvas, he shifted to the right to make room for her. He reached for his eye patch, but didn't immediately put it on, a fact that made her heart pump a little faster as she inwardly cheered. Then she turned toward the painting, and her heart slowed in shock.

Yesterday he'd spent most of his time revising his original depiction, correcting the lines and curves where he said his memory had failed to get the details precisely correct. When she'd looked at it afterward, she hadn't noticed anything dramatically different, even when Everett had pointed out all the places he'd made edits. It had looked like her before, and it looked like her after, just with more of her shoulders added.

Now, however, more color brought the image to life. Her skin carried a golden glow, and her lips blushed with a gentle pink hue. He'd even added the freckles that swathed her cheekbones and nose. Her hair might have given him the biggest challenge, but what she found most impressive was what he had accomplished with her eyes. Somehow, laughter sparkled in them. Warm, cheerful laughter. Perhaps it had to do with the placement of her brows or the tilt of her mouth. She didn't have the skill to recognize the technique he'd employed. All she knew was that when she gazed upon his work, one truth crystalized in her mind. He saw her.

"Everett . . . this is remarkable." She pivoted to face him, the awkwardness of using his first name overcome by her awe of his accomplishment. "It's me. Not just my face, but *me*."

"You are the remarkable one. I'm just painting what I see." The softness of his voice rolled over her nerve endings, leaving them tingling and sensitive.

Her breath hovered in her lungs, neither coming in nor going out as his gaze held hers. An invisible thread stretched between them, slipping between her ribs to wind around her heart. Neither of them looked away for a long moment until a distant bark from outside punctured her awareness and caused her to blink and dip her chin.

She stepped back, her pulse galloping. "Maybe I should hold a book during the next sitting," she said, more to diffuse the tension laying heavily in the air than out of any great desire to add a book to her portrait.

"Yes . . . right . . . good idea." Everett shuffled sideways and started tinkering with his palette and brush. "One with one of your covers. Show off a bit of your work. I thought of adding the library shelves as a backdrop as well."

"Papa would like . . . that . . ." She frowned. "Something seems to have Spartacus quite upset." Callista strolled across the attic studio to one of the windows on the front side of the house.

The deep bass canine rumbles had grown louder and closer.

Everett moved into position beside her, his eye patch back in place. Her nerve endings started humming again at his nearness, worsening when his arm brushed against hers.

"Looks like a visitor."

Ordering her attention to extend beyond the man next to her, Callista searched the path and spotted a figure on a large horse approaching the house.

Everett turned away from the window. Afraid of being seen or a lack of interest in the visitor?

"Whoever it is, Timens will send him away." Everett crossed back to his paints and began cleaning his brushes.

"I mean no harm," a voice boomed from below. A voice that even when distorted through window glass set her teeth on edge. "But you should know that if your dog attacks when I dismount, I'll shoot him."

Callista gasped and dashed for the door.

"Callista, wait!"

She paused with her hand on the doorknob.

"Let Timens handle it," Everett urged.

"You don't understand." She tugged open the studio door. "Ambrose Batton shoots animals for sport. Spartacus is in real danger."

Without giving Everett the chance to stop her, she ran down the stairs.

Chapter 16

Ambrose Batton? As in the man who'd been pressing his unwanted suit on Callista? The man they suspected of shooting Lightfoot? Everett charged down the stairs, envisioning another gunshot, only this time at close range. Bringing down the woman who had brought his heart back to life.

A roar built in his chest—her name—and begged for release. He clamped his jaw tight, imprisoning the impulse. He'd not embarrass her with overprotective possessiveness, even if that was precisely what pounded through his veins. He understood arrogant men. Shoot, he used to be one. They believed themselves invincible. Entitled to whatever they desired. They sought out weaknesses in their opponents and exploited them with no mercy. Everett donned a shield of icy disdain, determined to hide his weaknesses.

At least the ones that *could* be hidden.

If Batton was the kind of man Everett expected, he'd attack any available shortcomings, and Everett wore one of his biggest deficiencies on the outside for all to see. But today, his scars would serve as his screen, hiding his true weakness—Callista.

"Ah, Miss Rosenfeld. We meet again." Batton's overloud, unctuous greeting echoed through the entry hall, warning Everett that Callista had already made it past Timens. "You're looking quite fetching today."

"Spartacus. Heel."

Everett reached the first-floor landing and took a moment to steady his breathing and muster his composure. It helped that Callista had ignored the man completely and addressed herself not to Batton but to the dog.

Spartacus's barking mellowed, and Everett pictured the giant padding over to his newest friend and planting himself at her side. Everett planned to join him. He approached the entrance from behind the open door, taking a moment to size up the threat by peering through the crack between the door hinges.

"Please, miss," Timens urged in that fretful tone he used whenever things failed to follow the expected protocol. "Come back in the house." He left his post at the door and shuffled across the porch, arms outstretched toward Callista as if he could draw her back from where she stood at the base of the steps, mere feet from Batton's horse. "The master will not wish for you to be in harm's way."

"Harm's way?" Batton scoffed as he swung down from the saddle, strutted over to Callista, and propped a foot on the second stair, effectively blocking Timens's descent. He leaned forward and aimed a cocky grin her way. "Surely, you don't think *I* pose a threat." He spoke to Timens, but his gaze devoured Callista's face. "I hold Miss Rosenfeld in the highest esteem. In fact, I came here today to offer her my services."

Spartacus growled, obviously as distrustful of the man as the rest of them. Callista rubbed the dog's neck and hushed him, angling herself in front of the giant Mastiff as if she thought to protect *him.* Did she not understand that *she* was the one who needed protection? Her kind heart was going to get her into trouble.

"Mr. Batton." She spoke in a clipped, impatient tone that Everett had never heard from her before. "I believe I've made it quite clear during our previous encounters that I am not inclined to accept your offers. While I appreciate your kindness, I must decline."

"Decline?" He gave a forced laugh, but a muscle in his jaw ticked a warning of displeasure. "You haven't even heard what I'm offering yet."

Timens stiffened his posture and descended another step. "Please, sir. The lady has made her position clear. I must ask you to leave."

Batton speared the butler with a glare. "You ready to back up your inhospitable attitude with action, little man? Because you'll have to pick me up and plant me in the saddle to get me to leave before I've said my piece."

Timens bristled, at a loss for words. He held his ground, though, refusing to abandon Callista. Good man. Time for Everett to join the party as well.

Discounting Timens as no threat, Batton turned his disgustingly handsome face back toward Callista. "I heard your Sunday morning escort met with an unfortunate accident earlier this week. Such a shame." He made a *tsking* sound that lacked even a hint of genuine concern as he gave his head a wag. "A stray bullet, people are saying. Probably from an incompetent hunter. I hear your friend might lose an arm."

"You hear wrong," Callista snapped. "The doctor has assured us that Mr. Lightfoot will make a full recovery."

"But he won't be able to drive your buggy to church for you, will he? I know how important attending church is to you, and I would hate for you to miss even one service, so I'll be here bright and early on Sunday to drive you myself."

Everett stepped over the threshold and marched straight to the stairs. "That won't be necessary."

Batton turned, his scowl dark until he spotted Everett. He jumped back slightly, his foot falling from the step as his brows arched and his square jaw hung agape. "Great Scott, man. What happened to your face?"

"Probably the same thing that happened to your manners."

Batton's expression hardened, a spark of challenge lighting his gaze. Good. They understood each other. Everett strode down the stairs, placing himself between Batton and Callista.

Batton smirked. "You really are an ugly son of a gun, aren't you? I heard talk of a local monster in these parts. Thought it was just a bunch of kids exaggerating. Guess I was wrong."

Everett raised his left brow, refusing to rise to the bait. "Seems you're wrong quite often."

That wiped the smirk from his face.

"Miss Rosenfeld?" Everett kept his gaze locked on Batton. "Would you please take Spartacus into the house and keep him in the entry hall until after our guest has departed?" Everett figured she'd not want to leave if she believed the dog still in danger, so he'd send them both inside.

Timens's gasp and hurried footsteps told him breakable items currently residing in the entry hall would be gathered up with haste.

"Right away, Mr. Griffin." Callista moved behind him. "Come, Spartacus."

The furry beast jostled Everett from behind, and an odd look crossed Batton's face.

"Your name's Griffin?"

What did his name matter? Everett folded his arms over his chest and nodded. "It is."

Batton's gaze carved its way through Everett's face again, lingering over the eye patch. Then it traveled behind him, where canine toenails echoed on entryway tile and a certain beautiful woman likely peered out as she closed the door.

"Interesting." In a blink, Batton's expression switched from contemplative to cheerful. "Pleasure meeting you, Mr. Griffin." He tapped his hat brim then retreated to his horse and mounted in a smooth, practiced motion. "I'll be seeing you."

He gave a salute then reined his horse around and rode away, leaving Everett with a pit in his stomach that he couldn't quite explain.

Callista placed her latest finished volume into the book press and twisted the handle to tighten the overlarge screw that closed the iron plate on top of the book to ensure the newly-pasted leather cover learned its proper shape. After securing the press, she turned to view the fiction shelves behind her. Nearly full.

It had been almost a week since that awful visit from Ambrose Batton. A week full of tea times with Mrs. Potter, informative historical discussions regarding tapestries and ceiling frescoes from Mr. Timens, and daily visits to the library by Mr. Lightfoot, with his inexhaustible supply of amusing anecdotes. Unable to accomplish many of his duties with his arm in a sling, he'd alleviated his boredom by popping in on her, a happenstance she enthusiastically encouraged—for both their sakes. Yet, as each day passed, the end to her magical time with these dear people drew nearer.

How she would miss them! In the few short weeks she'd lived at Manticore Manor, they'd become like family. And Mr. Griffin—Everett—he'd become the dearest of all.

He hadn't needed her to sit for him any more after the first week of working on the portrait, but they still shared luncheon together every day up in his studio. He'd told her more about his family. His father the investment broker, and his brother Alex who'd followed in their father's footsteps. His mother's love of watercolors and her obsessive desire to be part of the top tier of New York society. Callista told him of her father's love of tinkering despite his laughable lack of skill with mechanical things. Of how she'd often wished she'd had a sibling to play with when growing up. Of how books had offered her escape and solace after her mother passed.

Things had been progressing so well between them that she'd even gathered the courage to ask about the circumstances surrounding his injuries. He'd been slow to respond at first, but he didn't shut her out. He eventually poured out the entire story. A beautiful woman with an ethereal voice. An innocent portrait sketching session that deteriorated into shrieking violence. A young woman's mental instability, and her family's desperation to cover it up.

Throughout the telling, she'd felt his regret and an occasional tinge of bitterness, but the pain that she'd witnessed in his artwork had been absent from his recitation. The wound was no longer open and bleeding. Any infection had been cleared away, leaving new skin to grow. A scar of *could have been* lingered, marking the place where his life had taken a drastic turn, but he was healing, and she praised God that she'd been able to play some small role in that process.

If only she could get him to stop hiding himself away. Yes, people could be cruel, but they could also be kind once they realized they had nothing to fear. She'd been thrilled when he'd offered to drive the household to church last Sunday, but he'd insisted on staying with the carriage. He'd kept his coat collar turned up and his hat brim pulled low while standing guard from the churchyard shadows, on a mission to protect her from Ambrose Batton. Who hadn't even put in an appearance, thank the Lord.

She'd longed to introduce Everett to the Poindexters, especially Wade. Show the boy that he had nothing to fear from the master of Manticore Manor and show Everett that friendship with the community was possible. But she'd sensed that Everett would balk, so she kept her introductions to herself. Perhaps Mr. Lightfoot could convince him to take that step after Callista left.

Her posture wilted. She didn't want to leave. But she had no choice. Papa needed her, and she missed him terribly. If only there was a way for her to have Papa and Everett in her life at the same time.

A knock on the library's door drew her gaze from the bookshelves to land on the man dominating her thoughts of late. Instantly cheered, she smiled in welcome and hurried forward.

"Everett!" She glanced down at his empty hands. "No *Allan Quatermain* this afternoon?" He'd finished reading *King Solomon's Mines* on Saturday and had started the second book in the series on Monday.

He held out his hands as if just realizing that he'd forgotten the book, then gave a shrug. "I thought we might do something different today."

"Oh?"

He came alongside her and offered his arm.

She gave him a quizzical look. "Something that requires an escort?" She tossed a sideways glance to the decorative clock that sat amid the shelves. "It's not yet five o'clock. I still have another hour of work to complete."

Something mischievous twinkled in his eye. "Not tonight. You have a party to attend, instead."

"A party?"

He tilted his head toward his extended arm, and all at once it hit her. He wore a suit. One exceptionally well-tailored to show off the width of his shoulders and narrowness of his waist. She glanced down at the plain blue work dress and white apron she wore every day and felt shabby in comparison. Nibbling on her lip, she reached a hand up to check her hair.

He leaned close and whispered a secret in her ear. "You look beautiful."

She rolled her eyes at him. "I look like I've been working in a bindery all day."

He smiled. "If this is what a woman looks like after she's worked in a bindery all day, you should write it up as a beauty regimen and print it in the *Ladies' Home Journal*. Debutantes will flock to binderies in droves."

She laughed at his ridiculousness. "Is this the legendary Everett Griffin charm?"

"I thought I'd dust it off for today's special occasion. Might be a bit rusty, though." His mouth twisted in an expression of self-deprecation she found utterly adorable.

After taking a moment to remove her apron and smooth the bodice of her dress, she slid her hand into the crook of his arm and allowed him to lead her from the library.

"And just what occasion are we celebrating?"

There was that twinkle again. "You'll see."

He turned toward the front of the house and led her to the formal parlor where she'd had her interview with Mr. Lighthouse all those weeks ago.

Everett slowed his step and gestured for her to enter the room ahead of him. The moment she crossed the threshold, a cheer rang out, and three beloved faces jumped into her field of vision.

"Happy birthday!"

Birthday? How had they known? Tears distorted her vision as joy flooded her soul. She glanced over her shoulder to find Everett beaming at her with little-boy hope in his eye. He'd done this. To please her. She smiled at him with all the love in her heart then opened her arms to embrace her friends, even starchy Timens.

Chapter 17

Another chunk of ice fell away from Everett's heart as Callista's warmth enveloped his makeshift family. Timens blushed and stammered as she threw her arms around his neck, but an indulgent smile softened the butler's oh-so-proper demeanor when he thought no one was looking. The man adored Callista. They all did. And she adored them right back.

Mrs. Potter drew her deeper into the room, but Callista twisted to peer behind her at Everett as she moved toward the seating area.

"Come on." The genuine joy radiating from her smile shot such longing through him, it required significant effort not to stagger backward from the force of the blow. "This is your doing," she teased. "There'll be no lurking in doorways for you, sir." She extended a hand and gestured for him to join the group, as if she considered his presence an enrichment and not a dutiful inclusion.

He caught Lightfoot and Mrs. Potter exchanging gleeful glances, but he ignored their romantic giddiness. This evening was about Callista and *her* happiness. Not his own. Although, he had to admit that, of late, his happiness tended to increase in proportion to hers.

"Here, dearie. You have the seat of honor." Mrs. Potter steered Callista to the upholstered armchair near the hearth where Everett often enjoyed sitting by the fire during the colder winter months. The chair dwarfed her petite figure, but he rather enjoyed seeing her there, her eyes crinkled with excitement.

Mrs. Potter perched on the edge of the nearby sofa, taking the side closest to Callista while Lightfoot sat to the housekeeper's right. He planted his foot on the rug and leaned forward to ensure he had an unobstructed view of Callista and the three packages waiting on the small table next to the arm of her chair. Timens took the seat opposite Callista on the far side of the rug, leaving the chair nearest her vacant. Everett lowered himself to the upholstered cushion, an attack of nerves suddenly drying his mouth. Thankfully, Mrs. Potter had no trouble taking charge.

"Mr. Griffin told us about the lovely birthday tradition you share with your father," his housekeeper explained, "and since the two of you can't be together this week, we thought to help you celebrate."

Callista looked to him, appreciation and delight beaming from her expression, and his insides turned to complete mush. "What a thoughtful gesture. Thank you!"

Her attention left him to visit each of the others, but it darted back to him before moving to the gift Mrs. Potter was handing her. A lovely pink hue tinted her cheeks as her lashes lowered, and his heart pounded with the vigor of a blacksmith's hammer. He'd seen looks like that before, but not since the destruction of his face. Looks of shy, feminine interest. Of attraction.

How was such a thing possible? Callista and he had formed a friendship, yes, and he knew her to be a woman of deep character who cared little for outward appearances. But for her to actually desire him? He couldn't fathom it. Being able to look past a disfigurement was one thing. Quite another to exhibit actual attraction. He had to be reading her wrong. Yet years of flirtation experience told him he wasn't. The dreams of love and family that he'd ruthlessly murdered years ago resurrected to dance within his chest—a dangerous dance of hope that logic insisted would only bring pain. However, as he watched Callista's eyes light when she untied the string around her first package, he found he didn't care two figs for logic's opinion. Only hers.

"Griff told us about your rule of not spending any money on the gifts," Lightfoot said as she pulled away the brown paper from the gift that must have been from the valet, seeing as how the paper folds were as crisp as the creases in his trousers.

Callista unwrapped a slender box that had likely housed one of Lightfoot's neckties. She took her time opening it, savoring the experience. Her indrawn breath acted like a magnet, pulling Everett closer until he leaned almost as far forward as Lightfoot.

"It's beautiful!" She removed a lace-edged handkerchief of fine linen from the box and held it up for all to see. "I've never owned anything so delicate."

Timens raised a brow. "What are you doing with a lady's handkerchief in your collection, Ray?"

Lightfoot offered a cocky grin. "A well-trained valet must be prepared for any eventuality, my friend."

But as he looked back to Callista, his gaze softened with a sentimentality that roused Everett's suspicions that something more than practicality had caused Lightfoot to hold onto that handkerchief. Could it have belonged to his late wife?

Callista folded the cloth neatly and placed it carefully atop its box. "Thank you, Mr. Lightfoot. It's such a thoughtful gift."

"I'm glad you like it."

Mrs. Potter handed her the next present, this one wrapped in a small, drawstring bag. Callista untied the bow, loosened the string, and tipped the contents into her palm.

"A pocket watch?" She looked up from the odd-looking timepiece—the front casing a different color than the back—shaking her head. "Oh, this is far too costly. I couldn't possibly accept."

Timens held up a hand. "I insist. Besides, it wasn't costly at all. I'm a bit of a tinkerer, you see. I enjoy taking clocks apart and putting them back together. I keep a box or two of spare parts on hand for when repairs are needed."

"A box or two?" Lightfoot scoffed. "You have an entire dresser drawer filled with cogs and gears."

Timens raised a haughty brow at his friend. "Not all of us are clotheshorses. I don't need a drawer for my extensive collection of cravats and neckties. Hence, I have space available to dedicate to more practical pursuits."

"Oh, yes. Keeping a drawer full of broken clocks is much more practical than storing gentlemen's fashion accessories."

Callista hid a smile behind her hand as Mrs. Potter shot a disapproving glare at the bickering pair.

Timens cleared his throat. "Anyway." He nodded at the gift in Callista's hand. "I can assure you there was no cost involved in the procurement of that watch. I pieced it together from remnants already in my collection. It's well within the rules."

"You *built* this watch?" Callista's awe brought a touch of red to the butler's neck. "My goodness! You're a man of hidden talents, Mr. Timens. I'm thoroughly impressed."

"Yes, well . . . one must have a hobby of some sort to pass the time."

"And here you are . . . *passing the time* . . . on to our dear Miss Rosenfeld." Lightfoot pantomimed the giving of a gift between the butler and Callista, earning a moan from Timens.

"I didn't think it possible, but your jokes have actually worsened since your injury."

"Perhaps my *timing* is off. Or maybe I'm too *wound up*. I'll try to put a better *face* on things in the future."

Timens rolled his eyes. "Must you torture us with your dull wit? This is supposed to be a party."

Lightfoot, eyes dancing, turned to Callista and winked at her. "I guess I need to *watch* what I say."

Timens groaned and Callista giggled, the sound so joyful and light even Everett found himself smiling.

Callista swallowed her laughter, though, and beamed a grateful smile toward Timens. "I will use this every day. Such a handsome and practical gift. I'll think of you every time I check the time." She shifted her skirt, placed the watch inside her pocket, then gave it a little pat.

"This one's from me," Mrs. Potter said as she passed a square box to Callista.

Callista lifted it up to her face and gave it a sniff. "Hmm. It doesn't smell like teacakes."

Mrs. Potter laughed. "Don't worry. I made plenty of your favorites for our dessert tonight."

"You mean I get teacakes *and* whatever is in this box?"

Mrs. Potter laughed softly. "Of course!"

Callista tore away the paper and lifted the lid. She glanced over at the housekeeper, her eyes wide. "Mrs. Potter . . ." Her words failed and she blinked several times as if fighting off tears.

"Go on, dearie. I know how much you admire it."

"But . . . your grandmother's teacup? This is a family heirloom. I couldn't possibly . . ."

His housekeeper squeezed Callista's hand. "You can, and you will. I have no children of my own to pass it on to, so when I'm gone it will likely just get lost in the back of a china cabinet somewhere, or worse yet, be thrown away because of its imperfections. But in your care, I know it will be treasured and appreciated."

Everett tried to peer into the box to see the object that had produced such sentiment. Callista must have noted his curiosity for she lifted the teacup and held it up for him to see. A delicate white cup rimmed in gold. Rather plain except for the gold wreath painted around the inside of the brim and the gold band around the foot. A small chip marred the top edge of the cup, making it impractical for drinking purposes, yet Mrs. Potter had deemed it important enough to cart all the way to Texas with her.

Callista wrapped it in the small towel that had been placed in the box for padding and replaced the lid. "I will take excellent care of it. I promise." She reached for her new handkerchief and began dabbing her eyes.

Everett slapped his palms onto his thighs and ran them down toward his knees. "I suppose I'm next."

Callista turned bright eyes to him, and his stomach twisted. He prayed she wouldn't be disappointed.

"I'm not sure I can compete with heirlooms and mechanical wizardry, but I have a couple humble offerings to present."

"More than one?" Callista raised her brows. "Goodness. I've already received such an abundance of blessings. You all are far too generous."

Callista deserved to be showered with more blessings than she could fathom. Birthdays, Christmases, random Tuesdays. *Anniversaries.* The tempting notion caught him unaware, nearly causing him to stumble as he strode across the room to where he'd hidden his first gift in a shadowed recess along the side wall. Thankfully, the stumble didn't turn into a full topple. However, it did serve the purpose of focusing his mind back on the matter at hand.

Collecting the easel, and taking care not to disturb the blue velvet cloth draped over the canvas, he carried it back to where the others waited. Callista had scooted forward to perch on the edge of her seat, her hands braced on the chair arms.

Her indrawn breath sent his pulse into an erratic rhythm.

"Oh." The word emerged like a sacred whisper. "Is this what I think it is?"

Not trusting his throat to open enough to let words pass through, Everett answered by removing the draped cloth with a flourish.

Callista gasped slightly, then rose to her feet and moved toward the portrait as if drawn by an unseen force. The others stood as well and approached, seeking a closer view.

Lightfoot broke the silence first. "Well done, Griff." He slapped Everett's back with his good arm. "You captured her essence perfectly."

"I agree, sir," Timens said. "Excellent work."

Everett nodded to the men, appreciative of their praise, yet waiting for the one who mattered most to render a verdict.

He'd spent hours on the details, desperate to get everything just right. An impossible task. For the more time he spent in her company, the more beautiful she became to him. A beauty too deep for paint to capture.

"I don't know what to say." Her voice trembled slightly, and he prayed it wasn't from disappointment. She turned to him. Her mist-filled eyes glimmered in the lamplight. "It's extraordinary." She wiped at one eye even as a smile arrived to brighten Everett's heart. "Though I still think you painted your model in much more flattering terms than she deserved."

Everett shook his head, her genuine humility as rare as her beauty. "I simply paint what I see."

"I don't know about that," she teased. "I own no yellow dress, yet somehow I'm wearing an elegant gown of sunshine."

"Well, that leads me to the second gift." And a gut full of tangled knots. He tipped his head toward Mrs. Potter, who had retrieved the large box from beneath the sofa while everyone had been looking at the painting. "I'm afraid we broke the rules on this one, but only a little. Everyone contributed something unique to bring it together."

Callista looked to the box then back up at him. "What did you do?" she whispered.

He shrugged, hoping she'd not guess how much of his heart resided in that box. "Only one way to find out."

Mrs. Potter laid the long box on the sofa cushions then motioned for Callista to seat herself next to it. She moved slowly, almost as if she were afraid the gift would vanish if she didn't sneak up on it. After gingerly lowering herself to the sofa, she took the package upon her lap and reached for the bow made of golden ribbon that stretched across its middle. She cast a tentative glance his way, as if unsure it was appropriate for her to accept whatever was inside. It probably wasn't, but he prayed she'd accept it anyway. Out of friendship if nothing else.

As she untied the bow, everyone crowded around. The lid came off next, and then she pulled apart the paper inside. He could tell the moment she saw it. Her eyes widened, her mouth trembled, and her breath caught.

"Everett . . . I mean, Mr. Griffin . . . I can't . . . It's too much . . . I . . ."

Mrs. Potter, who had moved behind the sofa, placed her hands on Callista's shoulders and gave her a reassuring rub. "This is from all of us, Miss Rosenfeld. Nothing improper about accepting a gift from a group of friends, now, is there? Mr. Griffin gave us the idea, and he covered most of the cost, but we all contributed. Mr. Lightfoot selected the style. Mr. Timens placed the order and retrieved it from the dressmaker. And I made a few alterations once I was able to compare it to your Sunday dress. Let's pop upstairs and try it on, shall we? It's only right for a lady to look her best for her birthday dinner."

Callista looked to him again, her eyes full of questions.

"Only if you want to," he said. "Dinner will taste just as delicious no matter what color you are wearing."

He offered a casual grin, one designed to hide how much he truly cared about the outcome, but he suspected he was out of practice. Either that or she could see the hope beating in his chest. For she beamed a smile at him as she finally lifted the confection of yellow chiffon out of the box and draped it across her lap.

"How could I not want to wear the most beautiful gown I've ever seen?" She turned to smile at Lightfoot and Timens as well. "Especially when all the gentlemen in attendance are decked out in their finery."

Timens sketched a bow. "You do us a great honor, miss."

"You are the ones who have done me the honor." Her gaze moved about the room, halting on Everett for a long moment before moving on to land safely on Mrs. Potter. "All of you. Truly. This is the most magical birthday I've ever had."

"It's far from over, Miss Rosenfeld." Everett waited for her attention to return to him. "There's at least one more planned surprise."

"Something else? Gracious. Any more delightful surprises, and I just might expire from the excitement."

He certainly hoped not. He'd been plotting for a week about how to let her know some of what he felt for her. A lot was riding on how this evening turned out. Possibly his entire future.

Chapter 18

"Just a couple more pins . . . and voilà!" Mrs. Potter grinned triumphantly as she stepped away from Callista's dressing table.

The housekeeper had pleaded to dress Callista's hair for the evening, and Callista hadn't had the heart to refuse the request. Though had she known her friend would spend the next thirty minutes tugging and twisting her tresses into a complicated style, she might have tried a little harder.

"What do you think?"

Callista tilted her head from side to side as she peered into the dressing table mirror. "I think you are nearly as talented decorating people as you are cakes."

Mrs. Potter's mouth hung slightly agape as she struggled to find an appropriate response. Callista laughed softly. "That was a compliment, I promise. You make the most beautiful petit fours I've ever seen."

Callista looked back to her hair and admired the soft draping around her face that exposed a center part before pulling back into an elaborate twist at the crown of her head. A few wisps had been left to curl around her face and along the back of her neck.

"I should have paid better attention to what you were doing," Callista said. "I've never tried anything more complicated than the serviceable bun I always wear." With no mother to instruct her on things such as hairstyling, and with no time to pour over fashion magazines, Callista's education in the fashion department was rudimentary at best.

Pleasure bloomed on the housekeeper's face. "I'll be happy to give you a few tips later, if you'd like."

"That would be lovely." Callista rose from her chair, clad only in her underclothes. "I suppose I best get dressed. We've forced the gentlemen to wait quite a long time."

Mrs. Potter waved her hand. "Pish posh. It's good for them to wait a little. Builds up the anticipation. Can't make a grand entrance without sufficient anticipation."

Grand entrance? Oh, dear. "We're just having dinner, Mrs. Potter. This isn't one of your fancy New York balls." Thank heaven. Callista knew next to nothing about dancing or society etiquette. "I'm just a bookbinder whose kind employer threw her a birthday party."

The housekeeper stepped close and placed a motherly hand on Callista's arm. "Sweet girl, you're much more than a bookbinder. You've become a treasured part of our family. Let us spoil you a little tonight. It will bring us pleasure."

Callista surrendered with a sigh. "All right. But I really don't care for being the center of attention."

The smile Mrs. Potter offered in answer carried a rather mysterious air as she moved to the bed to collect the beautiful new gown. "Well, you best prepare yourself, for when you walk down the stairs in this dress, no one will be able to look anywhere else. Especially Mr. Griffin."

A thrill shot through her at her friend's words, though she quickly dampened the warmth rising through her midsection.

Donning a pretty dress would not change the truth of who she was—a poor bookbinder's daughter with no social standing. Even if Everett did have feelings for her, his family would never approve. His mother especially, with how much she valued social prestige. Besides, Papa needed Callista. Without her help, the bindery would flounder. Family had to come first.

"Tonight is about you, my dear," Mrs. Potter said as she slid the confection of yellow chiffon and golden taffeta over Callista's head. "Tomorrow you can return to your life of bookbinding, but tonight . . ." She smoothed the fabric and turned Callista to face the full-length mirror standing near the washstand. "Tonight, you are a princess."

Callista sucked in a breath as Mrs. Potter moved behind her to do up the buttons at the back of her dress. She barely recognized the elegant creature reflecting back at her. The vee of her neckline left her throat and collarbone exposed as gathered chiffon draped across her body in Grecian style from each shoulder to the bottom of her ribcage. Another swath of gossamer fabric wrapped her waist before forming a bow at her back. Small rosettes at her shoulders connected the draped chiffon to the shiny gold taffeta of a slightly darker hue that formed the back of the bodice. Callista turned slightly to get a partial view of the back as Mrs. Potter finished the last hook. The bodice dipped in a vee along her shoulder blades, with chiffon rosettes decorating the edge. The chiffon overskirt lay in gauzy layers atop the taffeta and cascaded like a waterfall of sunshine nearly to the floor, leaving a slender border of golden taffeta exposed along the hem.

"Don't forget the gloves." Mrs. Potter held out a set of long, elegant gloves in a matching yellow hue.

"There are gloves, too?" Callista owned a small white pair she wore to church, but never had she owned a pair of dancing gloves that stretched above her elbows.

"Of course." The housekeeper smiled as she helped Callista slide her fingers into the appropriate holes.

"This really is a fairy tale, isn't it?"

Mrs. Potter chuckled. "Tonight is whatever you wish for it to be."

A dangerous thought. For giving herself what she wanted tonight would undoubtedly increase her heartache when the magic ended and reality returned with the sun.

'Tis better to have loved and lost than never to have loved at all. Tennyson's words filled Callista with almost enough courage to banish her nerves. She turned toward the door and pressed a hand to her fluttering belly. Hoping the poet knew what he was talking about, she set aside the cautions of tomorrow and stepped into the promised wonders of tonight.

"How long does it take to change a dress?" Everett grumbled as he prowled the length of the entryway for what felt like the fiftieth time since Callista had disappeared upstairs.

Was she having second thoughts about accepting the gift? It *did* stretch the bounds of propriety. In an effort to draw her closer, had he, in fact, pushed her further away?

Lightfoot stepped into his path and clapped his back with his good arm. "Easy there, Griff. You're going to erode the marble with all that pacing. Look." He nodded toward the butler sitting in an armchair, flipping through a copy of *Scientific American.* "You have Timens fretting about how he's going to repair the ruts in the flooring."

Timens glanced up long enough to raise an eyebrow at Lightfoot's ridiculous claim then went back to reading whatever article had captured his attention.

"I know you've been away from society for five years, but surely you remember how women like to linger over their toilettes before a special event."

"Callis—Miss Rosenfeld is not like society women." Praise the Almighty. "She's not one to fuss over her appearance." And yet, her appearance always stole his breath. Probably because there was no artifice involved. No vanity. No intent to lure or entrap. Just a simple, wholesome beauty that radiated from her kind heart.

"Ah. But you failed to allow for Mrs. Potter." Lightfoot nodded sagely as if his statement had unlocked some vast mystery. It hadn't. "Our matron of the manor sees Miss Rosenfeld as something of a daughter, you know. A young chickadee in need of feminine guidance. She's taken Miss Rosenfeld in hand, mark my words. In fact, you might not even recognize . . ."

Lightfoot's sentence dissolved as his eyes widened, and his jaw went slightly slack. Everett spun to face the staircase and immediately his lungs seized. Nothing so mundane as breathing belonged in the perfection of this moment. The vision descending the stairs could have sprung directly from his dreams. He'd known instinctively that she'd look glorious in yellow, but his heart hadn't been prepared for the reality of Callista Rosenfeld in a ball gown. She wore no jeweled necklace or dangling earbobs, but she didn't lack for accessories. The shy smile curving her full lips enticed like the finest perfume, and the rich depths of her glossy, dark eyes as they sought out his gaze outshone any polished gemstone.

The fabric of her skirt *swooshed* softly as one step after another brought her closer to him. Her gloved hand floated along the railing, barely grazing the polished wood. He imagined his arm replacing the balustrade, and pinpricks of delight rose along his skin.

Once his lungs recalled the mechanics of respiration, Everett moved forward to meet her at the base of the stairs. He extended his hand, his fingers trembling slightly in anticipation of her touch. Her lashes lowered demurely, and a dusky rose blush kissed her cheeks. Slowly, she placed her fingers in his, and her lashes lifted.

"Thank you for the dress, Everett," she whispered. "It's beautiful."

"You're the beautiful one." He lifted her fingers to his mouth and pressed a kiss to her gloved knuckles. "Happy birthday, Callista."

Her shy smile blossomed into a dazzling grin. "The happiest."

His heart thumped with wild abandon, like the hooves of a deer bounding across the prairie and leaping into the air every few strides simply for the joy to be found in soaring. With her hand in his, nothing seemed impossible.

A ponderous voice echoed to Everett's left, making him aware of his butler's presence.

"Shall we go in to dinner, sir?"

Everett never took his gaze from Callista. "May I escort you, my lady?" He held out his arm.

Her fingers found their way into the crook of his elbow as if they knew the path by heart. "I'd be delighted."

So would he, if he could somehow convince her to become his permanent dining companion.

Everett seated Callista in the chair next to his as Timens and Mrs. Potter brought in a bevy of dishes and arranged them around the table. Callista exclaimed over each one, making his housekeeper beam with pleasure.

In keeping with the festive nature of the evening, his staff joined them at the table. A possible miscalculation on his part, since they all seemed determined to relate embarrassing stories from his youth. However, Callista's laughter combined with the fond way she gazed at him after each story—as if she longed to know everything about him—erased his humiliation and left him feeling rather euphoric. It helped that she readily shared stories about her own past, unafraid to poke a little fun at herself as well.

The finest company in New York society could not compare with the gathering at this table. Everett couldn't imagine why he'd ever coveted the superficial pleasure that came with wealth and prestige. Not when there was authentic joy to be had in the company of humble people who cared nothing for appearances, connections, or politics and everything for friendship, encouragement, and genuine amiability. A fellowship that fed the soul.

Dinner slid into dessert and dessert into coffee. Lightfoot and Timens slipped away as scheduled while Mrs. Potter distracted Callista with baking tips. Everett scanned the doorway every few minutes for his valet's signal. When Lightfoot finally appeared and sent him a nod and an annoyingly unsubtle wink, Everett nearly jumped from his chair.

Callista turned to him, tiny lines appearing between her brows. "Is everything all right?"

"Fine." He smiled and ordered himself to cease acting like an inexperienced youth.

He was Everett Griffin, for pity's sake. The American Adonis, charmer of women, and stealer of hearts. He'd lost count of how many ladies he'd captivated over the years. Yet, he'd never cared for any of them the way he cared for Callista. And he wasn't that shallow charmer any longer, nor did he wish to be. Not when he finally understood the power of genuine respect and ardent affection.

Callista was a priceless treasure, and not simply because she possessed the ability to see past his scars to the man beneath. She'd beguiled him with kindness, courage, faithfulness, and artistic sensitivity. Should her face ever be marred by tragedy—heaven forbid—his love for her would not dim, for Callista's true beauty emanated from her soul.

He extended his hand, and she fit her palm to his without hesitation or question.

"I have one final gift for you this evening," he said as he helped her to her feet. "If you'll return with me to the parlor?"

"Another gift? You've given me far too much already."

Yet he wanted to give her more. He wanted to give her everything.

Everett tucked her hand into the crook of his arm as they rounded the dining table and exited into the hall. "No money was spent in the procurement of this final gift, I promise. It falls well within the bounds of your birthday rules."

"Well, in that case . . ." She squeezed his arm and smiled up at him in a way that set his pulse to thrumming.

Timens stood in front of the closed parlor door and sketched a brief bow before opening the door with a flourish and ushering them inside. Callista's indrawn breath brought his attention to her face as she took in the changes that his men had wrought. Furniture had been moved to the edges of the room, rugs had been rolled up, and dozens of candles had been lit and positioned around the periphery. A warm glow filled the room, and hope unfurled in his breast.

"Will you dance with me, Callista?"

Chapter 19

Had she somehow fallen into one of her books? Callista slid her hand from Everett's arm and took a few steps into the room, soaking in the magical atmosphere of the parlor-turned-ballroom. The candlelight, the gleaming floorboards, the crystal vases refracting shimmering diamonds into the air, making it easy to pretend that pixies fluttered among them. She spun in a slow circle, taking in each delightful detail as dreams from her girlhood—dreams of fairy tales and handsome princes and happy endings—surged back to life within her breast.

"Will you dance with me, Callista?"

Everett's voice—deep, compelling, and a tad uncertain—drew her attention. His gloved hand extended toward her as he dipped in a slight bow. The hope shining in the vibrant blue of his uncovered eye beckoned her to his side, but a touch of reality dimmed the magic as she slid her fingers into his.

"I would love nothing more than to dance with you, Everett, but I'm afraid I don't know how. All I know of dancing is what I learned standing on my father's feet when I was eight years old."

His gaze warmed. "I know enough for both of us. All you have to do is trust me."

Callista's heart pulsed with new fervor as she squeezed his hand. "I do."

As if it had been pre-arranged, Timens crossed the room to a decorative cabinet that had been scooted away from the wall. A curved box sat atop the cabinet, a small crank handle extending from its right side. Timens cranked it as far as it would go, then gently opened the lid. Music spilled into the room as if Thumbelina herself conducted a tiny orchestra from inside the box.

"Oh, it's wonderful!" Enchanted by the music box, Callista tugged a chuckling Everett toward the contraption to investigate. "How does it work?"

Timens pointed to the metal arm extending from the center of the spinning disc. "The crank starts the motor, which spins the disc," the butler explained in the same authoritative tone he used when discussing the merits of Renaissance architecture. "See the tiny projections on the disc?"

She leaned closer. "Mmm hmm."

"Those pluck the pins on the musical comb—the wand extending from the center. Each of the pins is tuned to a specific pitch . . . which . . . ah . . . yes, well . . . I'd be happy to explain more about it another time."

Callista glanced up from the music box in time to catch the butler tugging on his collar.

"I believe Mrs. Potter requires my assistance in the kitchen. If you'll excuse me?" He strode from the room with enough haste to almost be considered a scurry.

"Well, that was odd." She turned her attention to Everett, who looked far too innocent not to raise Callista's suspicions. She raised a brow. "Did you send him away?"

He held up his hands. "I didn't say a single word."

"Uh huh." She wagged a finger at him. "You gave him one of your scary glares, didn't you?"

"Maybe. But only because the man has a tendency to explain things in far too much detail."

"I happen to like details."

Everett's gaze heated several degrees as he stepped closer and reclaimed her hand. "I happen to like *you* and would prefer dancing over an educational lecture on the mechanics of music boxes."

Callista swallowed, or would have if her mouth hadn't gone dry in that moment. Heavens, but her insides melted when he spoke in that intimate tone.

"What do I do?"

He positioned her left hand to rest on his shoulder then took her right hand in his left before splaying his right hand on her upper back. His touch was firm yet gentle, and when he closed the distance between them, her breathing took on an erratic rhythm that failed to match the swinging meter of the music box waltz.

Everett leaned close and murmured in her ear. "Imagine a square etched into the floor."

That liquid voice of his had her imagining plenty, but nothing relating to squares on the floor.

Focus, Callie. You don't want to look the fool.

"I'll step forward with my left foot at the same time that you'll step back with your right." He moved his foot, and she hurried to move hers out of his way. "Then we'll both step to the side, and finally, bring our feet back together at the opposite corner of our pretend box." He guided her through the motions, and she followed without too much difficulty. "Now it's your turn to step forward with your left while I step back with my right. Then to the side, and close. Excellent."

She looked up from staring at her feet and smiled, ridiculously proud of her feeble accomplishment.

His eye twinkled. "Now we'll try it in time with the music."

He led her through several squares, patient with her missteps as she learned the pattern.

"You're getting the hang of it," he praised. "Now look at me instead of your feet, and let your body rise and fall with the music."

"I don't know if I—"

"You can." His thumb stroked a line along her back, sending an array of delightful shivers coursing over her skin. "Look at me, Callista. Please."

Drawn to the insecurity hiding behind his seductive tone, she lifted her chin and looked him full in the face. This dance was as much for him as it was for her. He needed her gaze as much as he needed her trust, and she'd not withhold either.

"Do you promise to catch me if I fall?" she murmured.

"Always."

The music box played its song again, and together they stepped into the dance. They held to their small box for the first few bars but then Everett led her into a widening pattern that twirled her around the entire perimeter of the room. She stepped wrong several times, but he covered each error with his own mastery, tugging her slightly closer to him each time until mere inches separated them.

Worry slowly gave way to wonder as Callista ceased counting in her head and allowed the music and her partner to move her where they willed. Everett pulled other metal discs from the cabinet when he grew weary of hearing the same tune, and each song felt more magical than the last.

She lost track of how much time passed, but who cared for time when dancing in the arms of a dashing prince?

Finally, the music box wound down and Everett brought their dance to a halt. His hand slid up to capture hers where it rested on his shoulder. He brought it to his lips and pressed a kiss upon her knuckles. Her breath caught at the feel of his warm breath through her gloves, and the soft touch of his lips weakened her knees. Slowly, he lowered her hand to rest against his chest and held it directly over his heart. A heart she could feel beating with the same ferocity as her own.

"Callista . . . I . . . I've come to . . . care for you a great deal over the last several weeks."

His hesitant words tenderized her heart more than any polished charm could accomplish. "I feel the same." She dipped her chin, as shyness swept over her.

Goodness. What was she doing? He was her employer and far above her station. Admitting feelings for him was far from proper.

"All of you here at the manor have become the dearest friends to me."

He frowned slightly. "I'd like to be more than a friend to you, Callista. I'd like to court you and eventually make you my wife."

His wife? Oh, how could a dream coming true hurt so deeply?

"But, Everett . . . we are so different. You're from the cream of New York society, and I'm a poor bookbinder who didn't even know how to dance before tonight."

"Do you think I care about any of that?" His voice rose a notch. "I haven't lived in New York in more than five years, and I have no intention of returning. If the difference in our circumstances doesn't matter to me, why should it matter to you?"

"It matters because I don't want to be another barrier to you reconciling with your family. Family is important, Everett. And yours would never approve of me. And mine? Well, Papa needs me. I can't abandon the Rosenfeld Bindery."

"So you'd abandon me instead." His frown brought his scars into sharp relief.

Callista retreated a step, not because she was afraid of him, but because the fairytale magic was rapidly disintegrating and tears seemed imminent. Hurting him felt like taking a lash to her own back, but as tempting as it would be to try, she couldn't pretend their reality didn't matter.

Blinking back the moisture pooling in her eyes, she lifted the hem of her golden skirt and hurried for the door.

"Callista. Wait. I'm sorry. I—"

She paused in the open doorway and glanced back at him, unable to stop the tear that finally spilled over the edge of one eye. "I love you, Everett, but I love my father too, and right now, he needs me more than you do."

Everett strode toward her, and her traitorous heart longed to let him take her in his arms and erase her concerns. But Papa was too precious to erase, so she fled before she succumbed to temptation.

A knife slashed Everett's soul at the sight of that tear slipping down Callista's cheek. He opened his mouth to call her back but swallowed the words and forced his feet to forfeit their chase. She was leaving him. Not just tonight, but forever. A wounded roar built in his chest, clamoring for release. He wanted to howl out his pain, to scream until his throat was as raw as his heart. How could she say she loved him and then leave?

Lightfoot stepped through the doorway, a scowl etched into his face. "What did you do, Griff? Miss Rosenfeld nearly ran me down in the hall, *weeping*."

Everett's fist clenched of its own volition. "I acted quite monstrous." Sarcasm dripped from his words like dark molasses. "I had the audacity to ask to court her with the intent of making her my bride."

Lightfoot blinked, his expression growing quizzical. "What precisely did she say?"

Agitation growing, Everett prowled back and forth, his arms gesticulating as he recalled the disastrous conversation. "That she cared more for her father than for me."

Lightfoot raised a brow. "That's what you heard, but I seriously doubt that is what she said. Women can feel affection for both father and husband. One need not preclude the other."

"I know!" Everett huffed out a breath then pivoted to face his valet. Lifting a hand to his head, he rubbed at the headache that had started pounding behind his eyebrows. Forcing himself to set his hurt aside, he thought back over her words with a touch more objectivity.

"She said she couldn't abandon her father or their business and that my family would never approve of her. She didn't want to cause the rift to widen between me and my parents. That family was important. She said she loves me . . ." He let that memory sink in for one blissful moment before continuing. "But she loves her father too, and he needs her more than I do. Which is utter rubbish. I've never needed anyone more than I do her. She brought me back to life."

"But what does *she* need?" Lightfoot's quiet question stilled Everett's spinning mind. "I've heard a lot about what you need and what her father needs. But what does *she* need?"

Everett grabbed the arm of the nearby settee and toppled onto the cushioned seat as surely as if his valet had just gut-punched him. How had he not thought to ask that question? He'd assumed his love, his provision, and his name would be sufficient. But it seemed she required more from him.

She needed his patience. His understanding. She needed to be accepted by his family, or at least for him to find a way to assure her that she wasn't hindering his reconciliation. A reconciliation he'd done a poor job of pursuing to this point. She needed to be near her father, to be part of his life. Maybe she even needed to continue her bindery work. Everett had assumed that his financial status would relieve her of the burden of work, but what if she enjoyed that work? The creative expression. The sharing of something special with her father.

Lightfoot sat beside him on the sofa and knocked his leg against Everett's knee. "Tonight need not be the end of your quest to win her hand, Griff. It can be the beginning. But only if you are willing to set aside what you want in order to become the man she needs."

Chapter 20

Everett didn't come read to her in the library the following afternoon. Callista hadn't really expected him to, not after she'd rebuffed his courtship proposition. She smoothed the endpapers over the glue on her last cover of the day, her heart aching. If only she could write an ending that would allow her and Everett to be together. Like Jane and Edward. Elizabeth and Darcy. Cinderella and her prince. But those who lived outside the pages of novels could not craft their futures with pen strokes and wishful thoughts. They must bear the fetters of reality as they hobbled forward one step at a time, making choices that affected not only themselves but those they loved.

Not all endings were happy in this fallen world. Papa lost Mama. Everett bore scars. Society withheld acceptance. Love was a powerful force, but it couldn't conquer *every* problem. Not until the day Jesus returned and took them to the perfection of heaven.

She checked for any stray glue then, after finding none, closed the cover and placed a stack of finished books on top so it would dry without bubbling or warping. Callista glanced at the handful of books on the corner of her worktable, waiting for their final fitting. Four. Only four books left until Everett's collection would be complete. Tomorrow would be her last day at the manor.

How she would miss this place! Mrs. Potter's tea parties. Mr. Lightfoot's funny anecdotes. Mr. Timens's precision. And Everett. She fluttered her lashes in a desperate bid to wave off the tears that rose to flood her eyes. No! She would not cry. She had too much to be thankful for. The blessing of new friends. Earnings from an important commission that would keep the Rosenfeld Bindery financially afloat. A reunion with her dear papa. The honor to have experienced love with an amazing man. A man who taught her to dance and who read to her in a voice as deep and silky as melted chocolate. A man who poured his soul into his paintings, holding nothing back as he used the talent God had given him to convey woundedness alongside hope. A man who loved books as much as she did and could appreciate a woman's professional skill. A man who valued her heart more than her face.

A man she would never forget.

Drat. At this rate she was going to take flight from all this lash flapping.

Lifting her apron to swipe it across her eyes, she glanced at the mantel clock. Dinner wouldn't be ready for another hour. Plenty of time for a nice, long walk. The fresh air would do her good. Clear her head, if not her heart.

Callista pasted a smile on her face before entering the kitchen. Mrs. Potter glanced up from chopping potatoes.

"Finish early today?"

"I did." Callista slowed as she passed the stove, taking a moment to breathe in the tantalizing aroma of baking yeast rolls. "Mmm. I never tire of that smell."

Pleasure lit the housekeeper's face. "The rolls will be ready in about ten minutes. Hang around, and I'll let you snitch a warm one."

Callista gasped in feigned shock. "Why, Mrs. Potter. What would Mr. Timens say? Snitching rolls before dinner?"

Mrs. Potter pointed her knife as if it were a finger. "My kitchen, my rules."

"Well, in that case, I'll be sure to cut my walk a little short. A warm roll sounds absolutely heavenly."

The housekeeper winked. "I'll set one aside for you."

"Thank you."

"Be sure to take Spartacus with you," Mrs. Potter called as Callista pulled open the back door and stepped outside.

"I will."

Or she would have, if she'd been able to find him. She called the dog several times as she set out on the path that meandered down to a small stream about a half mile from the house, but he never came. Must be off chasing a rabbit or facing down a feral hog. He did love to exert his dominance over the local wildlife. Callista smiled, though her lips wobbled a bit. She was going to miss him too. Her gentle giant. Fierce on the outside and tender on the inside, just like his master.

Who she was *not* going to cry over.

Straightening her shoulders, she lifted her chin and lengthened her stride. To further distract herself, she began singing a hymn in her mind, matching her steps to the marching beat of Fanny Crosby's *To the Work*. The lyrics proved an excellent reminder of the satisfaction to be found in a life of kingdom work. Laboring for the Lord, for family, for the benefit of others was a noble endeavor. A life with purpose. A life she'd always assumed would be hers. Meeting Everett didn't change that. It might have changed *her*, but it didn't have to change her path.

A cool breeze blew against her face, refreshing and invigorating her spirit as she strode toward the copse of live oaks that marked her destination. She brought Papa's face to mind and focused on how happy she'd be to see him again. To hear his voice. To feel his embrace. They'd been apart far too long.

Bending beneath the branches of the nearest oak, Callista stepped into the shade, but before she could fully straighten, a scratchy burlap sack jerked over her head. She screamed and grabbed at the oversized bag, but whoever held it forced it down over her arms, pinning her hands to her sides.

"No! Please! Let me go!" She struggled, desperate to break free.

But her captor refused to relent. In fact, he hauled her straight off the ground and flung her over his shoulder. She landed so hard, the air was knocked from her lungs. Stunned, Callista fought for breath as the man ran through the brush, carrying her as if she were no heavier than a toddler.

Once she could breathe again, she kicked and writhed, but all that earned her was a stinging slap across her backside.

"Quit squirmin', or I'll have to knock you out."

She stilled. Not out of obedience, but out of shock. She recognized that voice.

Ambrose Batton.

His desk full of wadded-up epistolary rejects, Everett read over his eighth and, hopefully, final attempt.

Mother and Father,

I have done you both a disservice by neglecting to write for such an inordinate length of time. Please forgive me. I fear my spirit was wounded more deeply than my face, and it has taken me quite some time to climb from the mire of self-pity to consider what pain I might be causing others by my actions. Or inactions, in this case.

Alex has kept me informed of some of the family news. I understand your first grandchild is set to arrive this autumn. How strange to think I will soon be an uncle! Mother, I'm sure you've been buying out the stores on the Ladies Mile to prepare for the blessed event.

Father, congratulations on securing the Jefferson contract. Alex mentioned in his last letter that society buzzed over the news for a week. I'm thankful the Griffin name is in the papers for all the right reasons this time around.

As it turns out, I have some news of my own to share. I've met the most extraordinary young woman. One who possesses a blindness to scars and an immunity to beastly manners. How she came to enter my life is a miracle I still don't fully comprehend, but one for which I thank the Almighty on a daily basis. She has the most cheerful, courageous spirit I have ever encountered and a heart so warm it has thawed the ice within my breast. I feel things for her that I have never felt for another, and I have reason to believe she holds some level of fondness for me in return. Unfortunately, she is reluctant to accept my suit because of the difference in station between us. She worries that my family will not accept her humble pedigree, and being very close to her own father, she will not pursue a relationship with me if doing so would worsen the estrangement between me and my family.

Her name is Callista Rosenfeld, and she is a book binder, a talented one. Mother, you would appreciate her artistry. She has recovered my entire literature collection. She and her father own a small bindery in Denton, Texas—the Rosenfeld Bindery. (I'm sure Father will conduct inquiries.)

I plan to seek her hand in marriage. I don't know if she will have me, but I am asking for your approval as a gift I may present to her to demonstrate my dedication to removing the barriers that stand between us. I invite you to pay a visit as well, should your schedule allow.

I've included a sketch of Miss Rosenfeld so that you might more easily picture her in your mind. You will note that she is quite a beauty, but her character and temperament outshine the fairness of her face.

I look forward to your reply.

Your son,
Everett

His gut churned as he folded the letter and sketch together and slid them into an envelope. Would his parents give their consent to his marriage plans? Would they even respond? He doubted they would deign to visit. They hadn't done so in the last five years, after all. Father's schedule didn't allow for time away, and Mother likely believed Texas to be overrun with warring Commanche, brazen outlaws, and despicable desperados. A smile twitched at the edge of Everett's mouth. Even contemplating a visit to the Wild West would likely send her into a fit of the vapors.

Of course, his parents might have written him off by now. His smile flattened. A son stained by scandal, best left forgotten. Even if that were the case, he hoped they would at least send a letter to inform him that they didn't care what he did with his life so long as it didn't touch theirs. That would suffice for his purposes. Surely, they would afford him those few crumbs.

Yet . . . he missed them, and hoped that, perhaps, they missed him too. At least a little. Ah, well. Time would tell.

Everett scooted back the desk chair in his chamber and rose to his feet. He checked the time on the clock on the dresser top behind him and groaned. He was late. Forty minutes late. It was nearly time for dinner, and he hadn't made an appearance in the library for their reading date.

Fool. She probably thinks you're avoiding her.

A growl rumbled in his throat as he snatched his copy of *Allan Quatermain* from his bedside table and charged from the room. He should have paid better attention to the time. How could he woo Callista if he neglected their friendship? He'd thought the letter would only take a short while to compose, but he'd obviously underestimated the time it would take to fish the right words out of the murky pond of his own hurt and regret.

Everett pounded down the stairs then took a few seconds to calm his pulse and find a smile before striding into the library.

"Sorry I'm la—"

Callista wasn't there. His chest tightened as the emptiness of the room threatened to spread inside him as well.

Calm yourself. She hasn't left you. Not yet. She's simply not in the library.

He spun and hurried to the kitchen. "Mrs. Potter!" His growing sense of urgency fed his volume. "Have you seen . . . What is it?"

Mrs. Potter, Lightfoot, and Timens all stood huddled by the back door, eyes wide, conversation frantic.

Lightfoot separated himself from the others. "Thank God you're here, Griff. I was just about to fetch you."

Everett's gut clenched as he dropped his book and letter onto the table and moved forward to intercept his valet. "Callista?"

"She decided to take a walk before dinner."

Mrs. Potter hurried forward, hands strangling the corner of her apron. "I told her to take Spartacus with her, but he must not have heard her call. When the dog showed up at the back door without Miss Rosenfeld in tow, I feared something had happened. I sent Mr. Lightfoot out right away."

Everett's temples began to throb. "Ray?"

"I walked down to the creek to check on her. That's her favorite spot, you see, but it's possible she walked elsewhere. We can't know for sure."

"What did you find? Spit it out, man!"

"She wasn't there, Griff. But I found something else. Boot prints. Large ones. Hoof prints too."

Everett's world tilted, and he had to grasp the table edge to steady himself. A man and a horse had been on his property without his knowledge. Watching his house. His people. Watching Callista.

He shoved away from the table, his hands fisted and ready for battle. "He took her." The very idea scalded his heart like boiling oil.

"Who?" Timens asked.

"Batton." Everett stalked past his butler and grabbed the rifle from above the back door. "I'm going after her."

"But you don't know where she is," Lightfoot said.

Everett turned and speared his friend with a glare. "Then I'll tear the entire town of Graham apart until I find—"

Spartacus's bark at the front of the house cut off his sentence. Everett ran through the house, gun in hand, and threw open the front door.

A boy in his teens stood a few steps away from the porch, quivering, his gaze locked on the Mastiff.

"Please don't let your dog eat me."

"Spartacus, heel."

The dog obeyed, trotting over to flank Everett at the base of the porch. When the dog retreated, the kid turned his attention to Everett, taking in not only his face but his fury.

"Who are you?" Everett demanded.

"Wade Poindexter, sir. I-I work with my pa at the coaching inn. I-I think M-Miss Rosenfeld is in trouble."

Everett strode forward, his glare hot. "What do you know?"

Wade backed up a step but lifted his chin. "S-She told me you were a good man. That y-you weren't the b-beast everyone says you are. But maybe she was wrong."

Maybe she was. Everett sighed and relaxed his stance, then turned and handed the rifle off to Lightfoot who had come to stand beside him.

"Sorry, kid. We just found out she was missing, and . . . I'm a bit . . . on edge." More like completely over the cliff and plummeting. He needed a lifeline, and he might have just alienated the one person willing to throw him a rope. "You did right coming here. It was a brave thing to do, considering my reputation. I want to find Miss Rosenfeld and make sure she's safe. What makes you think she's in trouble?"

Wade leaned forward. "I'd just delivered a package to the Conroe place and was back on the road when I caught sight of a man riding through the trees to my left. Recognized his horse right away. Only one big palomino like that in the area, and Mr. Batton rented him the day after he arrived. I wouldn't've paid him much mind except there was something big draped across his lap. Something that moved. I only got a quick look, but I'm sure it was a woman's legs kicking through white petticoats. I know Miss Rosenfeld doesn't care for Mr. Batton or his advances. I heard her tell my ma that she wished he'd leave her alone. That peacock don't seem the type to take no for an answer, though. Makes me worry he might have decided to take what he wanted whether she was willing to give it or not."

God protect her!

Everett swallowed the quickly swelling lump in his throat. "Which way was he headed?"

The kid turned and pointed. "North. He rented Henderson's hunting cabin when he first came to town. Probably heading there."

"Will you show me the way?"

Wade hesitated for a heartbeat then gave a sharp nod. "I'll do it. For Miss Rosenfeld."

Thank you, God.

Everett glanced over his shoulder. "Timens, saddle a second mount for the boy. I'll ready Enbarr."

Timens hesitated. "Shouldn't we report the abduction to the sheriff?"

"No time. Every minute she's in Batton's grasp increases the chance that harm will come to her. I won't risk her well-being."

And he wouldn't stand around arguing, either. Everett claimed his rifle from Lightfoot then took off at a jog, surprised when Wade matched his steps.

"I know my way around horses, sir. I can saddle my own mount."

Everett nodded, appreciating the kid's speed.

Every second counted, and he didn't want to waste a single one.

Chapter 21

Batton's rough hands slung her down from his shoulder and deposited her on the floor. Blind and disoriented, Callista collapsed to her knees and scrabbled to free herself from her burlap prison. The slam of a door spurred her to desperate speed, but her panic made her clumsy. Her hands fumbled until Batton grasped the top of the sack and yanked it off her head, taking several tufts of her hair with it. She bit back a yelp and blinked away the tears pooling in her eyes. She'd *not* give him the satisfaction of seeing her cower. Pushing to her feet, she brushed a fallen lock of hair from her face and glared up at him.

"Welcome to my cottage, Miss Rosenfeld." He sketched a bow as if she'd just stepped from a fancy carriage and strolled into a ballroom. "Do you like it?" He swept his arm in an arc to encompass the room. "I use antlers in all of my decorating back home, so I immediately felt at ease here. Isn't it cozy? I even brought a few specimens from my personal collection. Always nice to have a sentimental item or two when traveling."

Callista scanned the room, hoping to find an escape option or available weapon, but the décor he bragged about practically jumped from the walls. Dead animals stared at her with glassy, unseeing eyes. The mounted heads of several bucks with large antler spreads encircled the room, interspersed with two boars with tusks and several birds with suspicious dark spots on their underbellies. A coyote with bared teeth breathed down her neck from the wall at her back. She scooted sideways, bumping into a table. A coiled snake with large fangs toppled her direction. She squealed and batted away the venomous creature as Batton's dark laughter echoed off the rafters.

He bent over and plucked the stiff coil from the floor and settled the taxidermic snake back on the table. "I see you found one of my pets. I killed this one with my bare hands." He stroked the scaled head. "It tried to sneak up on me a few years ago while I was stalking a moose. I spotted him, took him by the tail, and whipped him—*boom*—just like that." He waved his arm in her face and gave a vicious flick of his wrist. Callista flinched. "Snapped his neck instantly." Batton's prideful grin turned Callista's stomach. "He travels with me now. A trophy of sorts. I do like pretty trophies." He stroked her cheek with the backs of his fingers.

Callista jerked her face away from him. "I'm nobody's trophy."

He laughed, the sound hollow. "With that face and figure? Honey, you were *made* to be a man's trophy." Batton snatched her wrist and dragged her deeper into the room. "And the perfect bait."

She dragged her feet and struggled against his hold, but her efforts didn't slow Batton in the slightest. "Let me go!"

"I don't think so, sweeting."

He tossed her roughly into a hard wooden chair then wrenched her arms behind her. A cord of some sort coiled around her wrists and pulled tight. As soon as he stepped away, she tugged and squirmed, trying to pull a hand free, but the cord held fast.

"The more you struggle, the tighter the noose will pull," Batton warned as he moved from behind her and collected a second chair.

Callista stilled. She'd not be able to escape with him watching her so closely. Better to bide her time and wait for him to leave the room before trying to free herself. What she wouldn't give for the scoring knife she'd been using just an hour ago. She'd have to find something else to use to cut her way free. Thankfully, she had an entire room filled with fangs, tusks, and teeth. If she could just figure out how to get to them.

Batton placed his chair directly in front of her and took a seat. "That's better. Now we can converse like civilized people."

"Civilized people don't abduct their company and bind their hands."

He raised a brow and ran his gaze down her form in a way that made her face heat in shame. "I could treat you with much less civility, my dear, and quite enjoy myself in the process. You'd do well to remember that."

Callista's mouth dried as her heart pounded in her chest.

Batton rose and hovered over her. One by one, he pulled the pins from her hair. When one refused to pull free of her tangled tresses, he forced it with an unsympathetic yank that brought tears to her eyes.

"There we go. That's better."

He arranged her hair over her shoulders, creating a wavy dark curtain she longed to hide behind. But he tucked the curtain behind her ears, leaving her exposed to his view. Was he preparing her to be mounted upon his wall? A pretty, lifeless trinket to proclaim his prowess?

"Can't have our bait looking scraggly, now, can we?" He smoothed her hair with his hand as if he were stroking a hound. "Everett Griffin has a weakness for beautiful women." He circled to stand in front of her, crooked a finger beneath her chin, and lifted her face. "*You*, in particular, I'd say, judging by the protective way he rushed to your side when I paid my last visit. That's going to make this all the sweeter."

She jerked her chin away from his touch, earning a chuckle from her captor.

"You know, when you first told me who he was, I thought I'd just lie in wait and shoot him like I did his interfering manservant." Batton flipped his chair around and straddled it. "But then I realized that a quick death was too easy for Everett Griffin. He needs to suffer for his sins. Slowly and painfully."

Callista's breathing grew shallow, and her head began to spin. Ambrose Batton had shot Mr. Lightfoot. Why? A picture rose in her mind of Mr. Lightfoot rescuing her from Batton's overbearing presence after church that first Sunday. And his protective hovering every Lord's Day thereafter. Had Batton shot Mr. Lightfoot because of *her*? Nausea roiled in her stomach at the thought.

And what of Everett? Merciful heavens! Batton sounded like he wanted to tear him apart piece by tiny piece. Was it some kind of deranged jealousy? Maybe if she convinced him that there was nothing romantic between her and Everett, he would let go of his vengeful plans.

"Mr. Griffin is my employer. Nothing more." At least nothing that would endure past her final day in his employ. "I've been rebinding some of the books in his library. That's all. Any protectiveness you think you noticed was merely his sense of responsibility toward an employee in his household. He has no claim on me, nor I on him. In fact, tomorrow is to be my last day. I'll be heading home this weekend, never to see Mr. Griffin or his staff again. There's no need for you to harm anyone else from Manticore Manor. They have nothing to do with what has transpired between you and me."

Batton smirked. "Leave it to a beautiful woman to assume everything is about her." He rose from his chair like a panther rising from a crouch and stalked forward. "I've been hunting Everett Griffin for five years, Miss Rosenfeld. Chasing lead after dead-end lead. Until last year, when a friend of mine mentioned seeing a piece of art in a Houston gallery bearing the signature of the very man I'd been trying to run to ground. I've been scouring Texas ever since, working my way systematically north through this oversized territory, determined to flush out my prey. I discovered you, instead, but thanks to a providential twist of fate, you've led me straight to my quarry." He smiled, and the look in his eyes sent shivers slithering over her skin like a hundred venomous snakes. "If it wasn't for you, my dear, I might never have found him."

"Henderson's cabin is at the end of that trail." Wade pointed to where the overgrown path disappeared into a group of trees.

Everett nodded and pulled his rifle from the saddle scabbard. "Thanks for showing me the way."

He set his jaw, trying not to imagine all the ways the next few minutes could go horribly wrong. The sum of his battle experience had been gathered from ballrooms and books. He knew nothing of gunfights. And while he and his brother had sparred in the boxing ring with enough regularity to keep in shape, he doubted Ambrose Batton would honor the Marquess of Queensberry rules.

"You better head back." Everett lifted his chin in the direction of the main road. "I doubt this will be a peaceful discussion."

Wade steered his horse's head around. "If it's all right with you, I'll keep the horse and ride back to tell my pa what's happening. I know your man went to fetch the sheriff, but the inn is closer than town, and Pa can help. He grew up in these parts and knows back ways into places I've never been."

"Fetch him. I'll be grateful for whatever help he is willing to give." And if Wade was racing back to the coaching inn, he'd not be in the line of fire. "Miss Rosenfeld is my top priority, though, so I'll not be waiting on him. Spartacus and I will do the best we can on our own."

Hearing his name, Spartacus drew his nose away from the ground and cocked his head toward his master.

Everett waited for Wade to head off in the opposite direction, then signaled with his hand for Spartacus to advance. "Let's go get her, boy."

Spartacus barked and loped down the trail. Everett followed, scanning the trees for danger as they approached a cabin backed up against a rocky hillside. It seemed a frontal assault would be the only option.

Whatever happens, Lord, keep Callista safe.

Heaven knew he was no Allan Quatermain. His marksmanship was mediocre at best, and his tactical stratagem for this mission consisted of three axioms: hide when possible, avoid getting shot, and save the girl. His grasp of how best to accomplish those goals was pitifully thin, but he possessed an abundance of motivation. Not to mention an unseen ally who hopefully had a plan in place. The Almighty possessed a rather impressive record for any battle he chose to enter. Everett prayed he'd enter this one. For Callista's sake, if not his own.

While still in the trees, Everett dismounted and patted his gelding's neck. "Stay here, Enbarr. You're too easy a target."

He pivoted to face the cabin, only able to see one edge of the building through the cover of the trees. Spartacus had scouted ahead. Everett couldn't see him, which made him a bit nervous, but he dared not whistle to call the animal back. Hopefully, the heritage of generations of hunting dogs, war dogs, and guard dogs running through his veins would hone his instincts.

Rifle in hand, Everett darted forward, careful to keep a tree between himself and the cabin at all times. Until the trees ran out.

What to do? He had no doubt Batton was watching for him. He'd be a sitting duck if he stepped into the open. Which left him with only one option—talk his way through.

"Ambrose Batton!" Everett's voice boomed across the twenty yards of open space between him and the cabin. "The sheriff is on his way. Let Miss Rosenfeld go, and you have my word that I won't hinder your escape."

No bullets whizzed by his head. That was good. But there was no response of *any* kind. That made him nervous. Were Batton and Callista not in the cabin? The big palomino stood saddled near the corner of the building, so they had to have been here at some point. Everett stepped slightly away from the tree shielding him, his gaze glued to the front window, expecting a rifle barrel to poke beneath the raised sash at any moment.

Nothing materialized. He inched out a little farther, debating whether or not he should rush the cabin.

Just as he prepared to launch, the front door opened. Callista stood in the doorway, her familiar blue dress a beautiful sight. But a meaty arm wrapped around her midsection marred the view, as did the leering face above her head. The glint of a steel blade near Callista's neck stole Everett's breath.

"Gotta give you credit, Griffin," Batton shouted from behind Callista. "You found me faster than I expected. Too bad. I had hoped to have more time alone with your lady."

Everett's gut clenched so hard he was surprised it didn't crack a rib. "Callista?" His voice broke a little. "Are you all right?"

"She's fine for now, but she won't be for long, unless you do exactly as I say."

"No, Everett! Run! It's you he's af—" Callista's words cut off and visions of the blade cutting into her throat speared through his mind.

Everett charged out from behind the tree, caution forgotten. With Batton holding her with one arm and wielding a knife in the other, the man couldn't shoot. But he *could* hurt Callista, and that's what he did. His blade sliced into the tender skin beneath her chin, drawing a cry of pain that ricocheted through Everett's chest like a barbed ball bearing.

"Not so fast!"

Everett skidded to a halt a few feet from them. "Please. I'll do whatever you want. Just don't hurt her." If Batton wanted him, he'd gladly make the trade.

"Drop the rifle. And your sidearm. Set them on the ground and kick them away from you."

Everett did as he was told, then straightened with his hands in the air. "I'm the one you want, Batton. Let her go."

Everett's gaze darted to Callista. Her beautiful brown eyes glistened as she shook her head ever so slightly, still trying to get him to save himself. Her eyes pleaded, but he'd not leave without her.

"I'll let her go," Batton said, "but only after you suffer for what you did to my cousin."

His cousin? Everett searched his memory for any Battons that he might have known back in New York, but nothing came to mind.

"I've never intentionally harmed anyone, Batton. I don't know who your cousin is, but—"

"Lillian March." Batton growled out the name, and the force of his released rage dug the blade of his knife into Callista's neck, drawing her whimper. "My cousin is Lillian March. You destroyed her, and now I'm going to destroy you."

Chapter 22

A warm trickle rolled down Callista's neck. Blood. A wave of lightheadedness assailed her, but she shoved it aside. She couldn't afford to indulge any weaknesses. Not when the man she loved was in danger because of her. Why hadn't she just waited for Spartacus instead of walking on her own? She shouldn't have even left the house. If she'd been thinking of others instead of herself, she would have stayed in the kitchen with Mrs. Potter and helped with dinner. But regret wouldn't get rid of the knife at her throat, nor would it get Everett out of harm's way.

Think, Callie.

"You've got your facts wrong, Batton." Everett, hands raised, edged a step closer. "Look at my face, man. Lillian already destroyed me. She's the one who came out unscathed."

"Unscathed?" Batton's arm tightened around Callista's middle, making her ribs ache. "She's been sent to a private sanitorium in the Catskills. Shuttered away from society. From potential suitors.

Her delicate mind bruised and imbalanced because *you* sullied her!"

The flat of the blade dragged across the underside of her chin, the sharp edge slicing her flesh as Batton whipped the knife out to point the bloodied tip toward Everett. The agonizing sting took her by surprise. She cried out and tried to reach for her neck, forgetting for a moment that her hands were still bound behind her back.

"Callista!" Everett leapt forward then had to spin sideways to miss the slashing arc of Batton's hunting knife.

"I'm all right!" There'd been no gush of blood, so the cut must have been shallow, even if it did hurt like the dickens.

She blinked away the tears causing her vision to blur and focused on Everett. She could not let Batton use her as a weapon against him.

"I did nothing to Lillian," Everett insisted as he backed away from the blade, circling around to her left. "I offered to draw her portrait, that is all. She is the one who sent everyone from the room to get me alone and throw herself at me."

"Liar!" Batton dragged Callista from the doorway, prowling forward to stalk Everett. "You wanted to trap her. Force her to marry you to gain society's favor."

Callista stepped awkwardly, and Batton adjusted his grip around her waist. Something hard prodded her wrist. Something jutting from his gun belt.

"I'd never compromise a woman. Frankly, back then I wouldn't have had to. I had dozens of debutantes throwing themselves at me during every ball."

Was he *trying* to get Batton to attack him? Callista stilled. Maybe he was. Keeping the knife aimed at him instead of her. Leaving her all but forgotten. She moved her hands, running her fingers over the rounded hilt. Another knife? Twisting her wrist, she managed to clasp it. Now she just needed to find a way to pull it free of its sheath.

"You arrogant rogue. Lillian outshone all others that year, and you know it. You wanted her for yourself. Admit it!"

She scooted it upward, one inch at a time.

"Why are you the one coming after me, Batton? Why not her father? I'll tell you why. Her father knows I did nothing wrong." Everett lowered his hands, jerking one of his palms in an unnatural direction. Almost as if he were signaling someone to stay back.

Callista twisted her head toward the corner of the house and spotted a familiar canine face. *Spartacus!* If she could just get away from Batton, the dog would have a clear line of attack.

"Lillian's always been unstable, hasn't she?" Everett pressed. "That's why her parents kept her on such a short leash. Only presenting her to the public when they could control the environment."

"Lillian is perfection! The most beautiful woman ever to grace the ballrooms of New York. If I hadn't been on safari in Kenya when she'd made her debut, she never would have looked twice at you."

Everett's eyes widened. "You're in love with her."

Callista nearly dropped the knife she'd just worked free. Ambrose Batton in love? Surely not. If he was in love with Lillian, why was he flirting with every woman who crossed his path?

Leaning forward to create a bit of space between her and Batton's midsection, she worked at turning the small knife, hoping he'd be too focused on arguing with Everett to notice her tiny movements. She jabbed herself several times but managed to angle the short-bladed knife to saw at her bonds.

Everett barked a caustic laugh. "I'm no competition for you anymore, Batton. Go claim your enchantress with my blessing."

Batton jostled Callista as he stalked forward again. The knife fell from her grasp. It worked its way down her skirt to plop softly in the dirt. Praying she'd weakened the cord enough to slide a hand free, she twisted and stretched her wrists against her bonds.

"Her father refuses to grant permission. Gave some rot of an excuse about ensuring her fragility of mind isn't passed on to future generations. As if a man wants a woman for her mind. Beauty is what a man craves. Isn't that right, Griffin?" His voice changed. Less angry, more . . . menacing. "You took my Lillian from me. Only fair that I steal your beauty." He raised the hunting knife and positioned the edge directly in front of her right eye. "I think I might just make the two of you a matched pair."

"No!" Everett face paled. "Don't hurt her. Please."

Callista sucked in a breath and tried to stretch away from the blade, but Batton's chest was like a brick wall behind her.

"What did I tell you, darlin'? All he cares about is your pretty face."

All *she* cared about was getting her hands free, and she'd almost managed it. With her right thumb tucked, she could feel the slip of the cord straining over her knuckles as she pulled.

"You're wrong, Batton." Everett's voice softened and his gaze found hers. "Nothing that touches her face can dim her beauty. It radiates from her heart. Her heart is what I love. Her heart, her mind, her laugh, her spirit. That is where her true beauty lies."

His words were so sweet, she nearly forgot to keep working on her hands. As her fingers finally pulled free of the cord, she loosed the last of her inhibitions as well. "I love you, Everett." He deserved to know.

Batton growled and raised his knife, shifting the angle so the end pointed at her chest. "I can rid her of her heart, too," he cried.

"Spartacus!" Callista screamed for the dog at the same time Everett lunged for Batton's arm.

The deep bark of the Mastiff echoed like thunder as Spartacus charged forward, teeth bared. Batton shoved Callista to the ground and drew his pistol with his left hand as he fought off Everett with his right. Terrified he'd shoot Spartacus, or worse, Everett, Callista raised up on her knees, grabbed his gun arm with her newly freed hands, and yanked downward as hard as she could.

With Everett gripping one wrist and Callista the other, Spartacus launched at Batton's chest and knocked the large man flat on his back.

Batton roared, tearing his arm from Callista's grip as he fell.

The gun!

On top of Batton's chest, Spartacus snapped at the man's face. Having knocked Batton's knife away, Everett rose and planted a boot on the man's wrist, pinning his arm to the ground. Both of her defenders were easy targets for the gun barrel twisting their direction. Callista did the only thing she could think to do. She dove atop Batton's bending arm.

A blast of close-range pistol fire concussed Everett's ears. He flinched, instinctively ducking away from the sound. Until he spotted Callista on the ground opposite him. Unmoving. A dark stain spreading across the side of her dress.

"Callista!"

No, God. Please!

"Spartacus, stay."

Hopefully, two hundred pounds of canine weight would keep Batton pinned. Everett sprinted around the supine form of his enemy and dropped to his knees at Callista's side. Cupping her shoulder, he gently rolled her toward him.

Wide eyes met his, and her mouth opened as if she struggled to draw breath. "Gun," she rasped.

As her hips rotated toward him, he spotted the pistol and wrenched it from Batton's surprisingly lax grip. Everett twisted his torso and hurled the weapon away, the distant metallic clatter comforting as he turned back to Callista.

Cradling her in his arms, he pulled her to his chest and moved her away from Batton. "You're going to be all right, sweetheart." She *had* to be all right.

She leaned forward, a horrible wheezing sound rattling in her chest.

Had the bullet punctured her lung? He laid her on the ground a few feet from Batton and immediately searched for an entry wound, needing to staunch the blood. Red stained his hands as he searched the fabric of her dress for a hole. Worried his single eye was missing something, he tore the patch away from his weak eye, but still, he found nothing.

He pressed his hand against the bloodiest part of her dress, an apology on his lips, but she didn't flinch at his touch.

Where was the blasted wound?

Glancing over his shoulder to ensure Spartacus still had Batton under control, he spotted a small knife on the ground a couple feet away. He leaned over and stretched out his arm just far enough to grasp it. He'd cut her dress away. Find the wound and staunch the blood.

He reached for the fabric at her waist and fit the blade beneath a blood-stained pleat. Callista curled forward and touched his wrist. He stilled. Peered into her face.

"I have to find the wound."

She shook her head. "Not me," she said, her breathing beginning to ease. She pointed behind him. "Batton."

Not her? It took a moment for the truth to penetrate his panic. Slowly, he swiveled to face his foe and processed details he'd failed to note earlier. The large and still growing pool of blood by his left side. The bent arm that had been under Callista. The fingers near his waist. Fingers that would have pulled the trigger.

He shot himself?

Everett glanced back at Callista and found her beautiful brown eyes filling with tears as she stared at Batton. "I-I didn't mean to . . ."

Bending over her, he took Callista's face in his hands and turned her away from the gruesome sight. "You saved my life, Callista. Nothing that happened here is your fault. Batton pulled that trigger. Not you. Understand?" A tear fell but she gave a nod. "That's my girl."

He smiled and pressed a kiss to her forehead, treasuring the feel of her breath against his neck. She was alive!

Easing back, he sought her gaze. "I'll see to him. You stay here, all right?"

She wrapped her arms around her middle and nodded.

Not sure what he'd find, he kept the small knife in his hand and approached with caution.

"Spartacus. Down."

The Mastiff relinquished his perch and trotted to Everett's side. When Batton failed to spring to his feet, Everett patted the dog's head and gestured for him to go to Callista.

"Batton?" Everett stepped around the blood and drew alongside the man's shoulder. He crouched down.

Knife in his right hand, he gingerly placed his left on the man's chest. No movement. Batton's eyes stared at the sky unseeing. Everett bowed his head, his gaze traveling down to the wound in Batton's side. The bullet must have hit a major artery to bring about such a swift demise. Nothing could be done for him now.

Reaching up to the man's face, he closed his lids over his eyes. "May God have mercy on your soul." He murmured the standard prayer, surprised at how much he meant the words. As a redeemed beast in constant need of the Lord's mercy himself, Everett found he couldn't withhold it, even from his enemy.

Everett retrieved a blanket from the cabin and draped it over Batton's lifeless form then returned inside to wash his hands and face and find clean cloths so that Callista could do the same. He carried a chair out to her and arranged it facing away from Batton then tended the wound beneath her chin. It would leave a small scar, but thankfully not in a place where she'd be reminded of her trauma every time she looked in a mirror. Like he had been. Yet, even had Batton's knife marred her face, Everett doubted Callista would have hidden herself away as he had done. She had far too much zest for life to become a hermit. No doubt, she'd continue working at her father's side, serving the public, her smile as bright and friendly as ever. Only the hardest of hearts would fail to see the beauty of her spirit.

Perhaps it was time for him to leave his own self-imposed prison. To cease caring so much about what others thought of his face and help them see who he was as a man. A man who had put his beastly ways behind him after being tamed by love.

Callista hissed quietly as he made a final pass over her cut.

"Sorry." Everett winced with her. "After the sheriff arrives, we'll get you home and dab some of Mrs. Potter's salve on this. She's got a cure for just about everything in that cupboard of hers. I don't think this is deep enough to need stitches, but I'll bring in the doctor to confirm."

Her fingers pressed against his forearm. "Everett?"

He glanced down at her hand then up to her eyes. Eyes shimmering with tears. Tears he suspected had little to do with her injury.

His heart pounded painfully in his chest. "Yes?"

"I want to go home. I need to see my papa."

Something cracked inside him.

"I can take the last few books with me . . . finish them at the bindery . . . I'll bring them back, I promise, and you won't need to pay anything until the job is complete. I just . . . I need some time . . . I—"

"Shh." He covered her hand with his. "Of course you can go home. I'll make all the arrangements. Don't give it another thought."

She leaned her head forward, and he raised up on his knees to cradle her face against his chest, careful not to touch beneath her chin.

Moisture filled his own eyes as he held her to him. His beautiful Callista. The woman who had brought him back to life. She loved him. She'd said the words. He could still hear the echo of her vow in his mind, the sweet sincerity of it ringing pure and true. Yet at this moment, she craved the nurturing love of another. He wanted her to turn to him. Heaven knew that if Everett loved her any more, his heart would split apart at the seams. Nevertheless, love meant doing what was best for another, not seeking one's own happiness. So as much as he wanted to hold her tight, he knew he needed to let her go. He just prayed it wouldn't be forever.

Chapter 23

Denton, Texas
Three weeks later

"Callie, I'm ready for the text block. Callie?"

Callista jerked her gaze from the small window in the bindery workroom and twisted toward her father. "Sorry, Papa. What did you say?"

He nodded at the collected pages she held in her hand, the signatures and endpapers she'd finished sewing together not ten minutes before.

"The text block? I'm ready to wed it to the cover."

Wed. The word hit her with an unexpected jolt, causing her heart to throb as images of Everett rose in her mind. Memories flooded her senses. The feel of his arms about her as they danced in the parlor. His deep, mesmerizing voice reading to her as she worked. The way his beautiful blue gaze would light at the sight of her. His gentle care of her after that horrible day at the hunting cottage. The heartbreaking moment when they'd said goodbye.

She could still feel the press of his lips on her forehead and hear his whispered words of love at the coaching inn. She'd been too numb from the shock of inadvertently causing a man's death to appreciate the gesture as much as he deserved, but those words had been stamped onto her soul like a book title on leather, changing her identity from Callista Rosenfeld, book binder and daughter of Mordecai, to Callista Rosenfeld, the woman Everett Griffin loved.

Yet his love had not echoed in words alone but in his actions as well. He'd bought all the seats on the stagecoach so that she could enjoy a private ride to the Millsap train station with only Mrs. Potter and Mr. Timens as companions. The pair had accompanied her on the train as well, riding all the way home to Denton at her side. Mrs. Potter had wrapped her in a maternal cocoon, ensuring she had everything she needed—food, comfort, the blessed distraction of conversation. Mr. Timens had taken care of all her equipment-laden trunks with typical Timens efficiency. Never once had she worried about transporting the heavy items from place to place. Timens had strong men with luggage carts waiting for them at each travel juncture. For the first time in years, she allowed someone else to carry the load of bindery responsibility while she tended to herself. Time to heal, Mrs. Potter claimed.

She didn't feel healed, however. The numbness had eventually worn off, and Papa's unconditional love and acceptance had surrounded her while she'd worked through the grief, guilt, and anger wrought by Ambrose Batton's demise. Yet a hole remained in her heart, one that could only be filled by Everett. The man she loved but could never have. Not at the expense of her papa and his family.

Everett had whispered other words in her ear at the coaching inn that day. He'd told her not to ship his finished books to him. He'd pick them up in person. A pledge she'd clung to for three long weeks. A pledge yet to be fulfilled, despite the fact that Papa had received the full payment for Everett's library commission. Maybe Everett had decided seeing her again would be too awkward.

Maybe his feelings had faded. Maybe he'd realized that being together truly was impossible and decided to let her keep the books as a remembrance of their time together. A sweet parting gift to commemorate a love that could never be.

Papa's touch startled her out of her melancholy musings as he gently took the text block from her hands.

"Sorry, Papa. I'm not much help today, am I?" At this rate, the paste he'd applied to the board would dry before he had a chance to affix the pages to the cover.

He peered at her over his round spectacles, love and understanding radiating from his gaze. "You're helpful to me *every* day, Callie. Even when your mind is elsewhere." He winked at her. "But I think today you might prove more helpful manning the front desk." Waving the hand that had been recently freed from its plaster bandage and declared fit for resuming work, he shooed her toward the door that led to the front of the shop.

Callista hesitated, her failure to be a worthy assistant prodding her to make amends. "We get so few customers this late in the day, Papa. Surely, I'd be more useful back here. I can just listen for the bell."

He raised a brow at her. "But will you hear it? Seems to me your hearing's not as keen today as usual."

Well, she couldn't argue with that now, could she?

He chuckled indulgently as he nudged her from the workroom. "If no one comes in, you can enjoy some quiet reading time. Something lighthearted, though, hmm? Perhaps *Three Men in a Boat* by Jerome K. Jerome. I read it while convalescing and found it quite delightful. There's even a dog. Montgomery, I believe. His antics are sure to put a smile on your face."

She'd prefer a dog named Spartacus, but her papa was right. Enough with the doldrums. Moping helped no one, including herself. The Lord had provided sunshine, books, and a loving family. Reasons to rejoice abounded.

Callista strolled to the front of the shop, determined to set disappointments aside and focus on her blessings. She found her father's copy of *Three Men in a Boat* and quickly became engrossed in the comedic travelogue.

Absorbed as she was, it took a moment for her to register the sound of the bell as the shop door pushed inward. Using a blank sales receipt to mark her place, she quickly closed the book and pasted a friendly smile on her face.

"Welcome to Rosenfeld's Bindery, how can I . . ."

Her greeting dissolved like sugar in tea as she beheld the customer walking toward the counter. Tall. Broad-shouldered. Tawny hair flowing past those muscular shoulders in unfashionable waves. A piratical patch covered his right eye while the blue of his left shone with such vividness, she could not look away.

"Everett?" His name fell from her lips in a hushed whisper. She crept toward the end of the counter, the magnetic pull of her longings drawing her feet toward him before her mind could fully comprehend the ramifications of his appearance.

He'd come! Just as he'd promised. He didn't even wear a hat, as if shame no longer held any sway over him. Her heart sang at the thought.

The longer he stood staring at her without speaking, however, the more reality intruded. Nothing had changed about their situation. He was still far above her station, and she still wouldn't abandon her dear papa.

An older couple entered the shop, and their appearance yanked Callista out of the fantasy of Everett and into the reality of her profession.

She smiled at the stunning, silver-haired woman garbed in a well-tailored, sophisticated dress who stood slightly in front of a man wearing a dapper, dark gray suit. The man pulled a top hat from his head as he pivoted to close the shop door.

"I'll be right with you, ma'am." Callista returned her attention to Everett. "Mr. Griffin." The forced formality abraded like an itchy blanket. "How nice to see you again." *Nice* barely scratched the surface, but it would have to do until she could find a way to speak to him alone. "I have the books you ordered ready in the back room. I'll collect them for you right away."

She turned to leave, but he hurried forward and clasped her hand. "Callista, wait. Please. I'm not here for the books. I'm here for you."

A flock of startled hens would have fluttered less than her stomach at that moment. Oh, how she wished she could throw herself into his arms, rest her face against his chest, and breathe in his woodsy scent. But she couldn't afford to cause a scandal in front of witnesses, especially those of the wealthy, influential variety.

Cheeks flaming, she leaned close. "Shh. You can't say things like that in front of other customers, Everett. What will they think?"

He grinned at her. "They won't mind."

"Well, I mind. I can't have you ruining my reputation and the reputation of Rosenfeld's Bindery."

He tugged on her arm, reeling her in. She should resist, she really should, but she wanted to be in his arms so badly, she couldn't find the strength to break free. Once he had her close enough, he wrapped an arm around her waist and pulled her flush against his chest.

"I guess you'll have to marry me then. To save your reputation." He smiled like the rogue he once was, and she swatted his arm.

"Shame on you, Everett Griffin. You know very well I'd never marry a man for so paltry a reason." Her pulse raced at the very idea of Everett and marriage being mentioned in the same sentence, however. "I'll only marry a man I love and who loves me in return."

His gaze grew serious as his grip on her tightened. "Then marry me, Callista, because you own my heart, and I am lost without you."

Her eyes misted. "Oh, Everett." How badly she wanted to say yes. "I love you with all that I am. But what about your family? We can't just pretend their opinions don't matter. They'll never approve of me."

"I wouldn't be so sure of that." He loosened his hold slightly as he turned to address the couple behind him. "Mother. Father. May I introduce Callista Rosenfeld? She is the woman I wrote to you about."

His parents! Good heavens. Could she make a worse first impression? They must think her completely lacking in decorum. She pushed away from Everett, smoothed the apron draped over her third-best dress, and lifted a hand to her hair.

"Mr. and Mrs. Griffin. I—"

Everett's mother strode forward and embraced Callista before she could form a complete sentence. "You restored our son to us." The older woman's voice broke as she hugged Callista tight. "I thought I'd never see him again, but then you came, and now our family is mended." She pulled back and looked Callista directly in the eyes. "You have more than our approval, my dear. You have our deepest gratitude." She stepped back and lifted a lacy handkerchief to her eye. "Tell her, Bradley."

Everett's father stepped forward and dipped his head. "Quite right, Miss Rosenfeld. We couldn't be more delighted at the prospect of joining our two families. In fact, your father and I have been corresponding about a particular storefront in Graham that I've recently acquired. He thinks it will serve well as the new home of Rosenfeld's Bindery. And frankly, after seeing the exceptional quality of your work on display in my son's library, I am quite eager to invest in your family's company."

Hearing her father's shuffling step behind her, Callista closed her gaping mouth and spun to face the man who'd proven to be more secretly conniving than she would have ever guessed him capable. "You knew about this?"

His eyes twinkled, the sparkle made all the merrier by the sunlight gleaming on the wire rims of his glasses. "I did. Your young man wrote to ask for my permission to court you a fortnight ago—permission I gave quite readily, you should know. Even before his father hatched the wild scheme of moving the bindery to Graham."

"But, Papa. What about the clientele we've built up? We can't expect them just to follow us. Graham is lovely, but there are no colleges or normal schools there. How will the business survive?"

Papa's grin only widened as he cast a look past her. "Told you she had a good head on her shoulders, didn't I, Bradley?"

Everett's father chuckled softly as he moved to join them. "That you did, Mordecai." He turned to Callista. "Your father mentioned to me that his true passion has always been the artistic side of book binding, so I proposed that we change your current business model from catering to educational facilities where your focus is mainly on repairs, to a shop that specializes in custom designs for a more elite clientele. I can take samples of your work back to New York to entice new clients from among our acquaintances, and my wife can offer her artistic talents to customizing designs for clients based on their individual tastes."

Everett's mother moved to her husband's side. "Everett told me how you worked with him to create a custom look for his covers. I found the entire process quite intriguing. If I can take samples of the different stamps and embellishments you offer home with me, I think I could convince many of the ladies I interact with to customize covers for their personal libraries. I could send you sketches along with the books to be recovered, and you could bring our vision to life."

Callista blinked. Was Everett's mother actually *excited* about going into business? Weren't socialites only supposed to concern themselves with planning parties and the occasional charitable endeavor? She looked to Everett, who offered a small shrug that seemed to indicate he'd been just as surprised but had had time to get used to the idea.

He worked his way to Callista's side and placed his hand into the curve of her back. Warmth traveled through her in a delicious wave. How she'd missed him!

"Show her your sketches, Mother."

Mrs. Griffin blushed. "Oh, don't be silly. They are amateurish at best. It will take time for me to get my bearings with this new medium."

"Sketches?" Callista looked from Everett to his mother. "Of cover designs? I'd love to see them." She smiled, hoping to encourage the woman who just might be her mother-in-law one day. Besides, if this new business model was going to work, she needed to know that the designs promised would not be too ornate or difficult to reproduce.

"All right. But these are very preliminary." Paper crinkled as she pulled a folded sheet from her handbag. "I thought to do something feminine, thinking of what a lady of means might desire."

She unfolded a pair of pages and handed them to Callista. The first used leafy patterns to craft what could easily be interpreted as an English garden blossoming along the edges to form an oval in the center. An oval framing a single, perfect rose. The large petals cupped upward in delicate lines simple enough to be tooled in a rich, red leather. The second page showed a drawing of a book's spine, the design a less-embellished version of the cover, broken up into three sections, top, middle, and bottom, with space left for the book's title and author.

"These are *beautiful*, Mrs. Griffin. I can already picture this on mahogany leather with gold embossing."

"You don't think it's too ornate?"

"We might need to thin out some of the vines so that we don't lose the fine detail, but—"

"Hand over those sketches, Callie." Papa chuckled as he gave her side a poke with his thumb. "You have more important things to do at the moment." He cast a meaningful glance at Everett that sent fire rushing to her cheeks. He turned to Mrs. Griffin. "How would you like a tour of the shop, Mrs. Griffin? I can show you how to bring that very design to life."

Mrs. Griffin took his proffered arm without hesitation. "Bradley and I would enjoy that very much. Wouldn't we, Bradley?"

"Yes, yes. Lead on, Mordecai." Mr. Griffin raised an arm toward the back room. "Can't go into business with a man without seeing where he works."

The three made a production of leaving that would have been comical had Callista's belly not been a tangle of nerves. It didn't help that Everett left her side as well. However, he moved in the opposite direction, going to the front door and turning the sign to read *Closed*.

When he pivoted back to her, his roguish bravado fell away, and a sweet vulnerability entered his gaze. "Callista. I don't want you to feel trapped by any of this. I took a lot of liberties without asking your opinion. Lightfoot encouraged me to find a way to give you what you needed—a way to stay close to your father, assurance that you wouldn't impede my relationship with my family, a way to continue your craft, should you desire to do so. Yet, if you truly wish not to marry me, all the changes I've set in motion can be undone. Well, except for my relationship with my parents. I plan to continue corresponding with them and encouraging them to visit. Shoot, I might even work up the courage to visit them one of these days." He glanced down as he rubbed the back of his neck.

A mist formed over Callista's eyes, but she blinked it away as she rushed forward and flung herself into the arms of the man she loved. He caught her with ease, just as she knew he would. And when his palms splayed across her back and clasped her to his chest, she sighed in utter bliss.

Tipping her head up to him, she beamed a smile that reflected a mere fraction of the joy shining in her heart. "Of course I'll marry you. How could I not, when you found such a beautiful way for us to be together? My mind is still reeling, trying to believe all that I've seen and heard in the last few minutes. It feels like a dream. A magical, wonderful dream."

Everett bent his head to nuzzle the side of her face with his cheek. "The moment I walked through that door and saw you again, I thought my heart had stopped. I've longed for you every day we were apart, and yet somehow, I still wasn't prepared for the reality of beholding you in person. It seemed you'd grown even more beautiful, your smile brighter, your eyes more expressive, and old insecurities reared their heads. I feared that outside the enchantment of Manticore Manor, you'd see only a beast and want nothing to do with him."

Callista's heart panged at his admission. She leaned backward just far enough to get him to lift his head. Then, when his face was before her, she cupped his jaw with both her hands. His eye widened as she rubbed the pads of her thumbs gently over the bumps and grooves of the scars around his lips and cheeks.

"I've never seen a beast when I look at you, Everett. I've only ever seen a man. And as I've grown to love you, I've come to see a man equal to any fairy tale prince. Noble and brave. Generous and kind. Protective and loving."

A tear pooled at the base of his eye, making the blue iris shimmer with a brightness that melted her heart.

"I make my living by crafting beautiful book covers, but I know better than anyone that it's not the cover that makes a person love a book. A pretty cover might be admired and put on display, but it doesn't stir the heart. Only the story or knowledge captured within the pages can make one fall in love and return to a book again and again. Think of your Bible, the cover worn and tattered in places. Yet, I'd wager you value that Bible more than any of the other books in your collection. It's not the cover that inspires love,

Everett. It's what's inside. And the man I see before me inspires a love so deep, it will never run dry."

Stretching up on tiptoes, she slid her fingers around his neck and tugged his face close to hers. She fit her lips to his as her eyes fluttered closed. He startled, drawing his face slightly away from hers, but she shoved aside her embarrassment and pursued him. Wanting to eradicate his doubts and needing him to believe in her love. He held himself still and stiff, as if afraid he'd scare her away should he reveal his own passion. But he should know by now that she didn't scare easily. She brushed her mouth against his once, twice, three times. Her pulse picked up speed with each tiny stroke. Yet Everett remained frozen.

Perhaps she was doing it wrong. Never having kissed a man, she had no idea what to do or how long to prolong the encounter. So she pulled back slightly to search his face for any clues that might offer instruction. His eye was closed, his face a mask of concentration, as if he were memorizing every clumsy attempt she made. Surely, he knew more about kissing than she did. If he would just take the lead like he had when they'd waltzed.

"Kiss me, Everett," she whispered. "Please."

As if her words unlocked his self-imposed restraints, he unleashed his desire in magnificent magnitude. He pulled her tight against his chest and cupped the back of her head in one hand, holding her face at the perfect angle to accept his kiss. And what a kiss! His lips moved over hers with a hunger that stole her breath. Yet the kiss gave more than it took—rich in adoration, tenderness, and love. His long fingers set her nape to tingling as they tunneled into her upswept hair, and when he deepened the kiss, she gladly accepted his tutelage and returned his kiss with all the amazement and love blooming inside her heart.

A small growl rumbled through him as his mouth lifted then immediately returned for another taste. The sound had her smiling against his lips, joy springing forth like a geyser in her soul. Perhaps there was something to be said for having a husband with a few beastly tendencies. A lifetime of passionate kisses and a love as fierce and strong as the mighty manticore himself—she couldn't imagine a happier ending to their story.

Review Request

If you enjoyed *To Love a Beast*, please consider writing a quick review. Leaving a positive review is one of the best ways a reader can show their appreciation to the author. Reviews are also a gift to fellow readers as they search for stories they are likely to enjoy. Thank you!

About the Author

For those who love to smile as they read, bestselling author Karen Witemeyer offers warmhearted historical romance with a flair for humor, feisty heroines, and swoon-worthy Texas heroes. Voted #1 Readers' Favorite Christian Historical Author in 2023 by *Family Fiction Magazine*, Karen is a multiple award-winning author and a firm believer in the power of happy endings. She is an avid cross-stitcher, tea drinker, and gospel hymn singer who makes her home in Abilene, Texas, with her heroic husband who vanquishes laundry dragons and dirty-dish villains whenever she's on deadline.

To learn more about Karen's books and to sign up for her free newsletter featuring special giveaways and behind-the-scenes information, visit her website at karenwitemeyer.com.

More Texas Fairy Tales

Fairest of Heart – Beauty has been nothing but a curse to Penelope Snow, and this time it nearly kills her. Rescued by a Texas Ranger and seven retired drovers, she is given a chance at a fresh start. Too bad the honorable Ranger she fancies suspects her of being a jewel thief.

If the Boot Fits – What's a girl to do when the most interesting man at her matrimonial ball isn't one of the bachelors on her father's guest list? Hunt him down, of course, using the only clue at her disposal—the boot he left behind.

Cloaked in Beauty – A Pinkerton detective on a secret assignment. A missing heiress with a pet wolf. A dragon of a man hunting them all. Keeping her out of harm's way may be just as impossible as keeping her out of his heart. Little Red Riding Hood and Sleeping Beauty entwine for a romantic fairy tale adventure.

* 9 7 9 8 9 9 9 2 4 2 0 5 1 7 *